I0675356

SE JAKES

RUNNING

BLIND

A HAVOC NOVEL

RIPTIDE
PUBLISHING

Riptide Publishing
PO Box 1537
Burnsville, NC 28714
www.riptidepublishing.com

This is a work of fiction. Names, characters, places, and incidents are either the product of the author's imagination or are used fictitiously. Any resemblance to actual persons living or dead, business establishments, events, or locales is entirely coincidental. All person(s) depicted on the cover are model(s) used for illustrative purposes only.

Running Blind
Copyright © 2018 by SE Jakes

Cover art: L.C. Chase, lcchase.com/design.htm
Editors: Rachel Haimowitz, May Peterson
Layout: L.C. Chase, lcchase.com/design.htm

All rights reserved. No part of this book may be reproduced or transmitted in any form or by any means, electronic or mechanical, including photocopying, recording, or by any information storage and retrieval system without the written permission of the publisher, and where permitted by law. Reviewers may quote brief passages in a review. To request permission and all other inquiries, contact Riptide Publishing at the mailing address above, at Riptidepublishing.com, or at marketing@riptidepublishing.com.

ISBN: 978-1-62649-869-3

First edition
September, 2018

Also available in ebook:
ISBN: 978-1-62649-868-6

SE JAKES

RUNNING BLIND

A HAVOC NOVEL

RIPTIDE
PUBLISHING

This one's for J, for bringing it back.

TABLE OF CONTENTS

CHAPTER 1

HELL AIN'T A BAD PLACE TO BE

"**N**o one quits us—*you're a dead man walking.*"

Those words rang in Bram's ears for weeks after the beatdown by the Heathens MC that left him wishing he was dead, which was the point.

Lesson given, lesson received.

Rest and recovery, the docs kept stressing, when all he wanted was to put as much distance between himself and the hospital bed as possible. And he'd meant that literally, planned on taking the vacation that his supervisor suggested.

For your heath—to rest and relax, Parisi'd emphasized.

Which was bullshit, because Bram was ninety percent sure a one-percenter, violent motorcycle club wouldn't let him escape that easily.

But maybe that's just you being paranoid.

To the Heathens, he'd been a prospective member named Monk. In reality, he'd been an undercover ATF agent who'd infiltrated the club and served up evidence that resulted in numerous arrests and convictions, putting the Heathens in serious legal and financial troubles.

Bram knew at the outset that leaving an MC once he'd been patched in was close to impossible, and that vacating even a prospect position would put his life in extreme danger.

He'd expected the ATF to have his back, and he'd been wrong.

"The plan went to shit," was all Parisi would tell him. *"Heads will roll."*

Bram was no stranger to pain, but there were moments during his recovery that he'd actively prayed for death. Most of the time he'd refused to let himself focus on the broken bones and stab wounds he'd endured.

To say he was skittish these days was putting it mildly, and it was safe to say that the last place he'd wanted to end up was Shades Run and in the potential crosshairs of another notorious MC—and too close to the one that'd nearly killed him for comfort.

But for his younger brother, Linc, Bram was a goddamned sucker. Which was why he was headed there to see a man about a bounty, and to get a lead on Linc's whereabouts. Because Linc had been MIA for months, even after Bram's doctors had left him a series of messages regarding the state of Bram's health.

Linc was a lot of things, and he could flake on a moment's notice, but like Bram, Linc knew life or death. For him to have just not responded...

Fuck it. Bram refused to let himself go there again. He'd move forward instead and deal with Linc's disappearance.

Which was why, nearly a month after his near-death experience, Bram found himself sitting in a bar called Bertha's the night before his appointment with the bounty hunter from Shades Run, who obviously got off on dialing Bram's number a hundred motherfucking times a day.

Goddammit, Linc.

Bram couldn't say that enough. Wouldn't stop anytime soon. He'd put his own life on goddamned hold for Linc again. Their sister, Linnea, told Bram he was nuts to do so again, but she always said that. In two days, she'd be calling demanding to know why Bram hadn't gotten Linc back home yet, not giving a shit that there was now a fucking bounty hunter threatening to show up at his door because Linc had jumped bail.

Obviously, Bram had been listed as giving collateral for the bond ... and he'd done no such thing.

Goddammit, Linc.

Because Linc knew that Bram's address needed to remain private, a necessity of his job. The fact that Linc no longer gave a shit about Bram's safety was enough for him to get ass in seat and drive to Shades with minimal stops.

First, he'd convince the bounty hunter that he knew nothing about the goddamned bond. And from there, he'd find Linc, get his brother on the straight and narrow ... and then decide if he was walking straight back into hell.

Not a problem at all.

Now, Bram stared into his beer, thought about all the hotel rooms in all the cities and countries he'd been in over the years, some for work, a lot for tracking Linc's ass down and bringing him back. Trying to get him a real job. Trying to make him responsible.

Fuck it. He was getting drunk tonight. He downed the shot in front of him and half his beer, and the bartender was already sliding the bottle of Jack toward him, asking, "Ready for another?"

Bram put a couple of twenties on the counter. "Keep them coming."

"Sure thing. But this one's on the house—courtesy of Grayson." The bartender motioned, and Bram turned to see the same bouncer who'd looked him over in subtle appreciation at the door earlier now giving him an easy smile. Bram wondered what that must be like, because nothing had been easy for a while.

Maybe tonight he'd find *easy*, along with its friend, *lucky*. But not anytime soon, because this place was getting more crowded by the second.

This wasn't a biker bar, but rowdy enough. Linc would fucking love it here. Lots of bouncers, almost enough to egg on a guy who liked bar fights for the pure sake of a good bar fight.

Linc called them art forms.

Thinking about Linc made Bram take the next shot quickly. It burned beautifully going down, but as he brought the beer to his mouth to chase it, he caught sight of leather jackets bearing an MC's rocker and he almost goddamned lost it. His hand trembled and he put the beer down and forced himself to fucking breathe.

As Dozer, his friend from the ATF, would often tell him, *"Calm the fuck down, son—it's all going to be okay."*

But how? He went through the reasons in his mind, ticking them off, one by one.

These MC men aren't here for you.

He didn't know that for sure, but their rockers bore the Havoc symbol, not Heathens. And although Havoc were notorious motherfuckers in their own right, Bram knew that Havoc did not associate with Heathens.

Plus, you look different from your time with the MC.

Dramatically so from his two years undercover as a prospect. He no longer wore a beard or mustache, and his hair was grown out longer than the shaved look he'd rocked with the Heathens. He'd also worn contacts and dentures that changed the shape of his face and jawline, and he walked differently than his MC persona had.

Hell, short of plastic surgery, there was nothing else he could do but live. Because the other option was to kill himself before the Heathens found him, and he didn't go down that easily.

Your job is over.

But honestly, some of the shit he'd seen and done for the Heathens? He'd never, ever live it down—or be able to live with himself.

Which was why he did two more shots in quick succession, finished another beer in two gulps, and waved for the bartender to keep them coming. Because Bram was in the middle of MC-land. Because of Linc.

That could be the title of his life's story, or maybe more fittingly, on his tombstone: *Because of Linc.*

After two more rounds in a ten-minute time span, he was rapidly becoming a paranoid fucking drunk. He stood, conveniently forgetting the pain factor of healing bones and ligaments and ribs sans pain pill he'd refused to take tonight. He grabbed his side and tried to breathe.

It was then he noticed that he was surrounded by lots of black leather. It was only three bikers, but that was enough. His flashbacks started almost immediately, his breath coming in harsh pulls, and he heard the bikers murmuring around him.

And then a hand went to the back of his neck, a cool palm with a light but firm touch, and a graveled voice asked, "Do you need medical assistance?"

"Just stood too fast," Bram managed. He forced himself to glance up at the man whose broad body was too close to his.

He was tanned, which made his eyes look slightly amber. He also had a lollipop stuck in his mouth, and his hair was up in a partial man bun. He was big. Ex-military, if Bram had to guess, and even though the guy hadn't said anything more, his eyes shone with concern.

Bram told him quickly, "I'm fine," in response to his unspoken question.

"You don't seem it."

"Why would you give a shit?"

"I own this place. My insurance premiums go up if someone dies on the premises," the guy explained, and Bram stared at him, noting he'd smiled a little as he'd drawled his explanation. "Come on, let's get you some air."

"Don't know you," Bram muttered.

"People call me Sweet."

Bram turned that over in his mind as he registered Sweet's hand persuasively guiding him away from the crowds—and the other two bikers—and fuck, Sweet was taking him outside.

Sweet from the Havoc MC.

Bad motherfuckers. They were the kind of club even assholes like the Heathens wouldn't touch. So Bertha's was Havoc-owned, and Bram hadn't done any research on the place, had basically done the equivalent of running into a burning building, because he'd been so focused on Linc.

Now, Bram focused on putting one foot in front of the other without tripping. As soon as he reached the open air of the alley, he turned and pressed the big man to the wall in an attempt to stave off a possible beating.

He was supposed to fucking run after that, but he became mesmerized by Sweet's reaction—instead of getting angry, he took the lollipop out of his mouth and smiled broadly . . . wickedly. "Better this than the knife you've got."

Bram stared at him, trying to decide if his instincts were right or if this was about to earn him another beatdown. Because Bram's cock told him he wanted Sweet. He hadn't noticed it inside while the smell of leather was panicking him, but now he was pretty sure Sweet noticed it too.

Shit. Suddenly, he felt too goddamned sober for this and completely out of practice . . . but his body knew exactly what to do as his hand palmed the back of Sweet's neck, tugging him closer, diving straight into the possible death wish and exactly like his old self.

And Sweet? The guy was laying himself open to Bram, hand in his hair, the other hand on his hip, but Bram was the one crushing him with his weight, kissing him hard, making both of them breathless.

Neither of them complained. In fact, Sweet's hand snaked from Bram's hip to the front of his jeans, tugging his own pants open first, then Bram's in order to palm both their cocks in his large, calloused hand.

"Fuck," Bram groaned into Sweet's mouth as the stroking intensified. He let his teeth drag along Sweet's lower lip, almost bit him, and it made Sweet growl deep in his throat. His hips tilted, body arched as their dicks dragged together, all hot and silky with a little bit of slick.

His hands went to Sweet's wide shoulders to gain some purchase and allow his hips to rock to Sweet's rhythm while he let himself grow drunk on the man. "Harder. Faster," he murmured into Sweet's cheek before biting him on his exposed collarbone.

Sweet complied, hissing as Bram sucked hard where he'd bitten. "That's good, baby."

"Come on—want to come," he instructed the motorcycle man he should be fucking running from instead of thinking about getting fucked.

But it felt good to feel in control, even though Bram knew he wasn't controlling shit in this situation, including and especially not himself. Sweet allowed him to retain the pretension as the pleasure built up to unbearable levels, until his entire body was strung tight as a goddamned bow . . . until his balls pulled up and he shot with a shout against the hot skin of Sweet's neck, coming all over Sweet's hand.

Sweet came a second later, somehow still managing to half hold Bram up against him.

God, how long had it been? Months and months of his own hand, he realized as he tried to get his breathing under control. Because prospects in the Heathens fucked women—no bisexuals or gays allowed. So he'd turned himself into a goddamned monk—hence the nickname—and pretended he'd been wounded in battle so he didn't have to fuck indiscriminately.

Although he loved women, he mostly missed the goddamned weight, the pressure and brute strength of a man on him. Sweet had given him everything he'd asked for.

And Bram wanted more. It didn't matter that the alley was dark, empty. Menacing looking. Didn't matter that they were alone, because Bram bet there was a guard at the door and another at the mouth of the alley.

Which meant Bram was locked in, pinned down with this big, leather-wearing, flashback-inducing, amazing-tongued biker. Bram's way of surrendering. Putting himself in unsafe situations . . . seeing which way he came out. If he came out.

Near-death experiences had a way of fucking you up and letting you prove that you were over and over again. Self-preservation wasn't on the invite list tonight, as evidenced by the fact that he was clinging to Sweet like the guy was a lover not a fuck, and hell, Bram had kissed him like that too. While he blinked and stared at Sweet, he realized Sweet was staring back at him in much the same way, a silent acknowledgment that something had clicked . . . and that both men hated that it had happened but planned on silently ignoring it.

And just like that, the feeling faded and the hair went up on the back of his neck. Sweet kept his eyes on Bram's face as he asked, "Like what you see?"

Bram shifted and glanced over his shoulder as the bouncer named Grayson admitted, "Was trying for a piece of him before you walked in."

"How'd that work for you?" Sweet asked as Grayson approached Bram from behind.

"Figured it's working just fine now," Grayson murmured as he sandwiched Bram between him and Sweet. Bram's hands were still on Sweet, one on his neck and the other on his shoulder as Sweet's hand dropped lower still, traveling along Bram's hip to . . .

Fuck. Bram shuddered when Sweet cupped his cock again. Behind him, Grayson chuckled softly. The bouncer was definitely his type, but Sweet? More so. Rough and fierce, and Bram figured they'd be well matched in a fight. And Bram had been ready to fight for his life. Still was, but the thrill of the death-wish option? Still strong.

Sweet was in front of him, Grayson behind. Bram's jeans were yanked down roughly by both men in tandem and then, in a quick, practiced move, their positions changed but Bram's didn't. Sweet was behind him, Grayson kneeling in front of him, Bram trapped between them still. His palms were on the concrete, his fingers scrabbling against the rough to try to remain planted—and he'd be falling if not for Sweet's arms banded around his waist.

He heard the snap of a lube cap before Sweet's fingers breached him, rough and practiced, and Bram hissed against the invasion while instinctively pushing back into it. He heard the rip of a condom wrapper, and that's when he stopped thinking and just gave himself over to all of it.

Sweet shifted his grip, clutching Bram's hips, pressing Bram's body tight to his and Grayson's unrelenting suck.

Sweet was big, and when his cock thrust up into Bram's tight hole, Bram whimpered softly. That spurred Sweet to push harder, as if he knew Bram needed the pain, craved it. He was panting, hips pumping.

The bouncer was jacking him with his tongue and suction, playing with his balls, trapping him and taunting him in that quiet, dangerous alley with a quiet, even more dangerous man behind him, and Bram had never done anything this stupid when he was undercover.

But fuck, this was good. Better than. Between Grayson's mouth, Sweet's cock, and his ability to come more than once an hour, he was going to shoot harder than before.

He started shuddering in warning. Sweet murmured, "You can come in his mouth," and Bram couldn't have pulled out even if he'd wanted to—the bouncer wasn't letting go as the spasms hit, jerking the heat from his body. It forced Sweet to slam up into him, his dick caught in the vise of Bram's ass as it contracted from the orgasm, and Sweet put his head against the back of Bram's neck and allowed Bram to milk him to a climax.

Bram closed his eyes as Sweet bit his neck hard enough to leave a mark, and yeah, he was focused on the sensations slamming him from all angles. He was vaguely aware that his legs would've buckled if Sweet hadn't made sure to hold him carefully, that both men had waited for him, until he was able to wave off their offers to walk him back to the hotel . . . unable to shake the feeling that they watched him the entire time.

CHAPTER 2

PLAYING FOR THE HIGH ONE

The next morning, Bram was outside the bail bonds shop with its innocuous sign at exactly 9 a.m. He wanted to be the first one there, in and out, getting his information and then taking off to find Linc.

On waking, he'd been comfortably sore, oddly satiated and wound up all at once, and so he'd showered, checked out, shoved his bag into the trunk of his car and made the trip through the midsized city.

He didn't want to think about how much danger he'd put himself in last night . . . or how much he'd liked it.

He was addicted to the adrenaline rush danger provided, a moth to a flame—danger gave him a bigger, better thrill than any high ever could, but he was an addict just the same. Sub out fucking an MC president in riding distance of the MC that nearly killed him and it was the same thrill.

In a lot of ways, Bram was way worse than Linc. Bram just happened to end up in a job that made his risk-taking seem legit instead of stupid crazy.

Of course, when Linc had pointed this out to him, Bram had scoffed. But really, his baby brother was a smart guy. Too smart to be wasting his life wandering around.

Now, he pulled the door of the shop open and a bell jangled. As he approached the counter, a man walked out of the back room. "Name's Gypsy. How can I help you?"

He was big. Blond. Easygoing, or you'd be led to believe, but Bram knew better. "You contacted me about someone named Linc," Bram started, but Gypsy cut him off by putting one hand up while he rifled in a drawer with the other before slapping a contract down on the counter between them and pointing to the bottom of the page.

It took Bram mere seconds to process what Gypsy was showing him, another few to piece together what happened. Having dealt with Linc since birth, it wasn't that hard, and it was exactly what Bram had seen coming.

His forged signature was on Linc's bond form, which also stated that Bram had put his house up as collateral. So Linc had attempted to forge Bram's life away and instead of hanging around here and checking in, he'd run. "I didn't sign this."

Gypsy stared him down. "Not your signature?"

"Nope. And I have no idea who this Linc guy is." He'd played this game before. It often suited the brothers to pretend they weren't related. This time it was imperative. "Wouldn't you have already met me when I signed this?"

"Maybe I told him it was okay with me for him to bring it in with your signature instead. But I talked to you on the phone. I recognize your voice."

Bram groaned inwardly. Linc had learned to mimic his voice from an early age.

Gypsy continued, "You said you'd do anything to help—you even sent a picture of your license to show me the matching signature."

At least they didn't have the same last name—Bram had dropped his father's years earlier. But it was time to push acting to award-winning levels. "This can't be fucking happening to me."

"So either you produce Linc . . ."

"I don't know who he is."

"Or you pay me," Gypsy said in what was probably his most reasonable badass voice. A brow rose when Bram shook his head. "Or I take your house."

"Don't own one." As Gypsy's brow furrowed in confusion, Bram pointed to the address and mortgage information on the form. "I don't own this house. My neighbor does. I rent it. This is forged."

Gypsy folded his arms and looked pissed as hell. "How do I know you didn't do that?"

"You're the one who gave bond to a criminal and you're asking me? I don't have a record. My wallet was stolen last year, with my license in it." Bram leaned on the counter and realized that Gypsy was selectively hiding Linc's information, including his most current address, dammit. "Dude, I don't owe you this money. Which is good since I don't have it."

"*Dude*, I don't care if you have to sell your ass to make the money." Gypsy was staring at Bram in a way he knew all too well.

The bells attached to the front door jangled behind him and, judging by the look on Gypsy's face, another badass had come in, and that was one too many.

He heard, "Problem?" and Bram called, "I've got this," over his shoulder before the voice registered and the way-too-familiar graveled voice shot back, "No, you don't, if he's talking about selling your ass."

Bram turned to see Sweet. *Sweet*. With the lollipop. And the leather rocker.

"I'd be buying," Gypsy told them both, like he knew he was about to incite a riot and didn't care.

"I'm out of here," he announced.

"You can't just fuckin' leave," Sweet told him.

As Bram stared between Gypsy and the man in black leather, he saw Gypsy narrow his eyes to stare purposely at the bite mark above the collar of his T-shirt . . . and then followed his gaze back to the almost matching one Sweet wore before suggesting to Bram, "You can work it off."

Bram snorted. "Or you can find your own fucking skip before I turn you in for fraud."

Gypsy slapped his hand on the paperwork. "Your signature. Your money. Pay up."

"If I don't, what're you going to do? I don't have this kind of money." Granted, he did have it, in the form of a money order in his wallet, but he didn't see the need to pay up before he'd learned anything. "Besides, I'd never have signed for him because I don't fucking know anyone named Linc."

"This was faxed back from your number."

"I don't care how he did it—I guess he's a resourceful asshole."

"True that," Gypsy concurred under his breath.

"I'm not going to find him—do your job," Bram said.

Sweet leaned against the counter and said thoughtfully, "As president of this MC, I'm telling you that you're fucking with my club's business. If I was a betting man, Bram, I'd say you do know Linc—maybe he's an ex who did you wrong."

Sweet's words slowly filtered through Bram's brain.

President of Havoc? Fuck me. Because Bram finally put two and two together. Gypsy the bounty hunter was part of the Havoc MC. Had to be, for Sweet to be invested in Bram's business.

Fucking, fucking Linc. And fuck me for not noticing any of this last night.

Maybe he really did have a death wish . . . and more in common with Linc than he'd ever thought.

He took a breath and slid into his newest undercover role by impulse rather than design. Ah Christ, letting both men think he and Linc were an item wasn't a bad way to go—especially because Bram wanted them off the track . . . but there was an unexpected flash of jealousy in Sweet's eyes—so fast Bram would almost swear he'd made it up if it hadn't made his belly flare with a pleasant heat.

But before Bram could do or say anything more, his phone buzzed in his pocket—his sup's ringtone. "I've got to take this."

Sweet nodded and moved away to give Bram privacy. Gypsy retreated to the backroom, Bram supposed for the same reasons, and he was damned grateful.

Granted, both men had also moved to block the exits. "Hey," he said casually.

"Where are you?" Parisi demanded.

"Where I said I'd be," Bram said automatically, which was a lie. Why he'd felt the need to do that—twice now—to Parisi, the man who had his back above all else, wasn't something he could explain beyond a gut feeling. "What's up?"

Parisi sighed. "There's some chatter—"

"About me?"

"Heathens aren't letting you go as easily as we thought," Parisi admitted. "They're searching."

Bram's blood chilled. "How hard?"

"I'll play you the message."

As Bram listened, the message from his undercover voice mail began, "You're dead, fucker," and went downhill fast from there with, "I don't care if it takes the rest of my life. You killed my son. I'll find you and I'll make you pay. Best bet would be to kill yourself and take the easy way out."

The messenger was Bones, XO of the Heathens MC and one of the meaner motherfuckers Bram had ever had the displeasure of meeting. He had no doubt Bones would live up to his rep—he'd never made a promise he hadn't kept—and Bram had been there several times, forced to watch and not intervene as Bones made good on his threats.

"Thanks for that. Gotta go," he told Parisi.

"Bram, you just lay low and try to relax. We'll figure this out."

"Right. Let me know when you do. I'm on vacation." He ended the call and shoved the phone in his pocket, annoyed at how badly his hands shook.

Sweet was leaning against the front door, staring at him. "Rough call?"

"Nothing I can't handle," Bram lied. He was good at it because he'd been doing it his entire life, but suddenly, he was goddamned exhausted. His doctors told him to take it easy. His sup told him to take a vacation.

And now, his home had been compromised. His cover might've been compromised—at the very least, the Heathens weren't about to let him disappear off the ends of the earth. Hiding in Shades Run, with Havoc, seemed to be the best idea. But in order to do so, he'd have to at least admit one thing to Sweet about his identity.

Sweet had been fishing with the ex comment, and with that he'd given Bram the foundation for the idea that would help him stay off the Heathens' radar. "So, about Linc? There's been a misunderstanding."

Sweet pushed off the door and came closer, but his guard was still completely up, evidenced by his next words. "Yeah? What's that? Forgot you do know him after all?"

Bram admitted, "Linc's my younger brother, Sweet."

Sweet cursed, probably more so at being surprised than anything. "You look nothing alike."

It was true—Linc was blond to Bram's dark hair, and Bram was broader too. Swarthy, he'd been told, a rough, devilish look that always got him in trouble. Both he and Linc had a fluid sexuality, moving easily between women and men—it was all about pleasure. "Different fathers. But we grew up with our mom and Linc's dad. So now that I know he's missing, I'd appreciate it if you'd give me any info that could help me, and I'll find him and bring him back."

Sweet continued to stare at him, and Bram was left to wonder how deeply Gypsy dug into Linc's family tree to search out other family. "As enlightening as all this is, I can't let you leave. Especially now."

"Can't *let* me? I told you the fucking truth. You can't hold me hostage," Bram protested, but judging by the look in Sweet's eyes, that wasn't exactly the truth. And yes, Bram could easily overpower the two men—or make a damned good attempt to—but he had to be smart. Play it cool. Deal with his shit and Linc's.

And save your ass.

Sweet stared at him. "Did Linc really forge your information on the bail bond?"

Bram nodded. "I haven't been in touch with him for a month, and when I got all the messages, I figured I'd come and see what trouble he'd caused."

"Does that happen a lot?"

"The trouble? Definitely. The out-of-touch part, not so much," Bram told him honestly. "I know he liked being in Shades. He stayed put, and that's not like him. So yeah, I was hoping you might be able to tell me what he was doing while he was here . . . if he might've been in trouble. Because it doesn't seem like he'd leave willingly."

Sweet shrugged. "Minor stuff with the law. No problems with our MC."

That was vague. "But problems with another MC?"

"Minor stuff. It's done."

Shit. Bram forced himself not to react or ask anything more about the MC subject. He could get more out of Sweet—and he would—but this wasn't the way. "Since I'm already checked out, you got any suggestions of places to stay besides that shitty motel?"

Sweet's brows shot up. "No arguments about staying, then?"

"You said I couldn't go anywhere," Bram said easily, in keeping with his *don't have a care in the world* bullshit. "Besides, I want to see if I can get Linc to come back here and do the right thing."

That was definitely the right sentiment, because Sweet nodded. "What about work?"

"I'm on vacation."

"From?"

Bram gave a long-suffering sigh. "I'm in insurance. High-ticket items."

Sweet narrowed his eyes slightly. "So you're a hunter."

"You could say that."

"So if you're so good at finding, why not Linc?"

Sweet was good. Bram was equally so, especially when it came to letting the truth leak through his cover. "Linc's always been my kryptonite."

Sweet nodded. "Fair enough. As for a place to stay, Gypsy's got a loft above the shop. Head on up and let us figure this out."

It might be as ominous as it sounded, but Sweet's expression hadn't changed. And staying here wouldn't put Bram under Havoc's protection, per se, but he'd be watched. Out of the frying pan and directly into the fire, but hell, he'd lived through worse.

CHAPTER 3

DANCING WITH THE DEVIL

Sweet watched Bram take the key from Gypsy and disappear up the stairs and into the spare studio apartment. Gypsy switched the surveillance camera on so they could watch Bram, sans sound. Sweet silently regretted not pressing Gypsy to put that extra security measure in place.

"So . . . last night?" Gypsy asked casually as Sweet tore his eyes away from Bram, who was predictably searching the room for cameras and bugs.

"Yeah. Me, Bram. And Grayson."

Gypsy smirked. "So why'd you get so possessive when I mentioned his ass?"

Instead of answering, or wondering why himself, Sweet grunted.

"We're fucked," Gypsy muttered. "Some of us more recently than others."

"Just keepin' an eye on our money," Sweet managed evenly.

"You didn't know it was our money last night," Gypsy pointed out, a hint of anger in his tone.

"I know every fucking thing that goes on in this town," Sweet corrected. "Stranger rolls in and stays at that crappy-assed motel, I hear about it. He comes to Bertha's, has a panic attack, and he's got fresh scars all over him? Something's up."

"You followed him here," Gypsy seemed to realize, after a beat. "And you're reeling him in."

"He could go a long way to getting Linc back." Sweet knew Gypsy was equal parts devastated and pissed that Linc had run off. And if Sweet were a betting man, he'd have lost big on this one, because he was pretty sure Linc appeared to be settling down and settling into Shades for a good, long run.

Gypsy nodded. "Is he using?"

"No track marks. Ozzie went through his gear—" Sweet started and Gypsy interrupted him with, "And you fucked him for distraction purposes."

"Did what I needed to," Sweet told him, taking a lollipop from the bowl on Gypsy's counter. He'd quit smoking how many goddamned years ago and still felt the need to have something constantly in his mouth. "Anyway, Ozzie found prescription shit, but if you saw the scars . . ." He shook his head. "Makes sense."

"Linc never mentioned a brother. Just a sister."

"But he put Bram's name on your books."

"Never said brother. Said friend."

"People have all sorts of reasons why they do shit."

"Doesn't mean we have to get involved," Gypsy pointed out.

"I thought you wanted to find Linc?"

Gypsy's expression tightened. "Flight risk. Flaky. Not good for the club."

Yeah, flight risk. Flaky. And a motherfucking thief on top of it. Sweet didn't take kindly to anyone fucking with Havoc or their money. "So you're just giving up on him?"

Gypsy flashed a "fuck you" expression and it was probably only his respect for Sweet that kept him from lashing out. Instead, he put his head down and started going through his files.

"Gypsy—"

"Don't. It's cool."

But it wasn't, and he and Gypsy had both lost a hell of a lot over the years. Sweet'd been hoping that Linc was for real as badly as his friend, but Sweet was far more cynical and had the weight of the club on his back. And Sweet had been pissed at Gypsy for not seeing Linc for who he was—an unrepentant thief, first and foremost. Linc was an easygoing guy for sure, but he'd done major damage and Havoc had allowed it. Because he'd been former Army, because he'd been friends with Rush, who was with Havoc's XO and therefore a Havoc member . . . and because he'd been sleeping with Gypsy. *One of us,* some of the Havoc men thought.

Gypsy'd thought that too, until Linc skipped and Sweet discovered the shit with the credit cards immediately after. He hadn't told many of his Havoc brothers about the fraud since they all knew that Linc skipped on Gypsy—bail aside—and they were all pissed. No need to release the hounds for Linc, because that wasn't how you caught a thief.

Sweet needed bait. Something to hold over Linc's head. And currently that person was one floor above and probably far from an innocent bystander. "I won't let anything—or *anyone*—fuck with Havoc, Gypsy."

Gypsy looked him in the eye, translating Sweet's unveiled threat. "You don't have to say that. I know that. I won't either, Sweet. So we'll do what we need to do."

And just like that, they were back to an even keel. On the same page that violence might be the only solution for what Linc had put the club through. The way Sweet figured it, Linc would come back for his brother. Sweet wasn't entirely convinced Bram didn't know where Linc was, but even if he didn't, once Linc caught wind his family was embedded with Havoc, he'd get the message.

Sweet ran his hands through his hair as he stared at the camera Gypsy had up, which showed the main empty room Bram was staying in. The bathroom wasn't wired.

"I'll stay here tonight," Gypsy said.

"Don't bother. I'll be with him for tonight."

"Why not just fuck him back at Havoc?"

"Still vetting him."

"Right." Gypsy shook his head. "You never have any problems bringing your one-night stands back to Havoc, Sweet. It's only the important ones you keep away. And there haven't been many important ones at all."

That last line was said gently, with the right amount of reverence for what Sweet had loved and lost over the years. "He's not a one-night stand. He's Linc's brother. He's a lead," he said tightly, not sure which one of them he was intent on convincing more. "I'll be back soon and I'll make sure he's okay," was all Sweet could manage before he headed out the door.

He needed a ride to clear his head before he went back in to Bram, needed to get his equilibrium back, and fast. The attraction had been instantaneous. Bram was good-looking, but not pretty. His attitude screamed *tough*, so when he'd gotten up off the barstool and looked like he was about to lose his fucking mind, Sweet had been concerned. He'd seen enough vets with PTSD to know that the guy was having some kind of freak-out panic attack and that the physical pain etched into his expression had good reason to be there. While Sweet got Bram off, the scars told a story of their own, of Bram being beaten—and badly—within the last six months.

He'd fought hard battles himself and could smell bullshit a mile away, but with Bram, there was bullshit and there was truth, all balled up together. Sweet needed to know more. Wanted to, if he was honest. But he'd also learned long ago how to separate his personal life from Havoc. Bram was a means to an end, and knowing that he got off on the fight, Sweet easily figured out how to make himself indispensable.

So Bram was his bait. Linc's brother. Nothing more, nothing less.

Bram knew he'd made the right decision about the best way to both keep himself safe and find Linc. Protesting too hard against staying at Gypsy's would've set off suspicions, and Bram had already aroused enough of them. For the moment, he had a bit of their sympathy regarding Linc, but Havoc was all business, and they wanted their bond money. Bram was the best way they had of getting that, so keeping him close was good for all involved.

Except for maybe Bram, when all was said and done.

"Fuck me," he muttered, then shoved his bag onto a chair and sank down on the already-made bed. It was comfortable and clean—much nicer than the hotel, but in the long run, this would cost.

Maybe just his ass, but still.

He swept the place for any and all surveillance equipment and found a weak feed which undoubtedly supported picture but not sound. Still, he turned the TV on before taking his second phone out of his bag. It was time to make contact with someone from home who wouldn't turn him into his sup, so he slid into the bathroom, shut the door and hit a button to dial Dozer, one of his oldest friends from the academy. They hadn't partnered together, but they'd always looked out for each other on the QT.

Bram definitely needed that kind of discretion now, so he called the line the two of them used when they didn't want to be monitored the fuck out of by the agency. Which was basically all the time. "Hey, Doz, it's me."

"Buddy—good to hear you alive and breathing." Dozer's voice was a low, slow drawl. "I heard you broke out of the hospital and left for warm weather."

"Yeah, that's what I told Parisi."

There was a pause as Dozer digested Bram's words. "So, where the hell are you? You know, in case I need to visit."

Bram stared around the small apartment before answering, "Shades Run."

Dead silence and then, "You're fucking *kidding* me."

Bram blew out a hard breath. "Honestly, I'm still having the same reaction."

"I thought you were lying low?"

"I was. I am." Bram sighed. "I'm helping Linc."

"By killing yourself?" Dozer asked harshly. "You're too close to those MCs for my comfort. Where're you staying?"

No one knew where he was. That in and of itself made it a fucking stupid move, which was a big part of the reason he'd called Dozer. "I'm staying above this place called Gypsy's Bail Bonds. It's—"

"A Havoc-owned business," Dozer managed before cursing up a blue streak and ending it with, "Are you fucking nuts?"

"They don't know who I am. Not exactly."

"And they can't. Just keep your head down and keep in touch. If you go longer than twelve hours without sending out some kind of smoke signal, I'm sending someone in."

"Like who? I'm supposed to be on vacation."

"Jesus, Bram—how you've stayed alive all this time's a mystery to me. Twelve-hour check-ins, at most." Dozer hung up before Bram could argue. He set a few alarms on his phone so he wouldn't forget and unwittingly trigger a manhunt in his honor.

Then he stripped his shirt off and lay down on the bed, dove in and let himself drown into his newest role.

He slid into his undercover roles as easily as he pulled on a pair of jeans. He became who he was supposed to be—total immersion. He'd been pretending since he was little, pretending to be happy, pretending that his family was normal, pretending his stepfather didn't beat him on a regular basis. Anything to stay with Linc and not get tossed into the system.

Bram knew that foster care was a hell of a lot worse than what they'd had. And so the bruises were from being a boy, falling off his skateboard, and the broken bones from out of trees. He'd been quite the storyteller, talking himself into the military and then the ATF and then proving himself in several short-stint undercover stings.

Of course he'd caught the attention of the top brass. His last assignment before the Heathens was taking down a growing sect of white supremacists.

If he didn't become who his new ID said he was, if he didn't accept their mindset, he'd never be able to stop them. That wasn't simply a justification—it was a necessity. And once the job was over, the hatred, disgust, regret would come pouring out of him in wave after wave of guilt and shame. It didn't matter that he'd stopped them. Being forced to participate? Part of the job, but part of his pain forever.

It'd taken him a year to recover from that before Parisi approached him about becoming a Heathen MC member in order to take parts of their operation down from the inside.

There was no good way to eliminate the entire MC, but they could stop the guns and drugs that were hurting the surrounding communities.

The job had become all about putting out fires. And it made Bram tired as fuck, but no less committed.

For Linc? More committed than he'd ever been.

Composed, confident, he remained on the bed, not closing his eyes, but forcing himself to relax as daylight receded. He remained in the dark, even when he heard footsteps approaching moments before a knock on the door.

Sweet or Gypsy? A toss-up, but Bram's dick knew which one he hoped it'd be. *Motherfucking traitorous dick.* "Yeah?"

"Dinner."

He switched on the light before opening the door, still bare chested, to find Sweet with a couple of bags. "I didn't order takeout."

"Figured you didn't think about food." Sweet brushed past him and Bram subtly inhaled the scent of leather.

Fuck, it was nice. Didn't induce panic attacks like it almost had last night. Maybe using Sweet for some kind of immersion therapy wasn't so crazy after all.

He watched as Sweet put the bags down, then stared him. There was appreciation there, but as Bram suspected, it was coupled with more. He knew Sweet had noticed the scars last night and that he had questions. Under the harsh florescent light, the fresh scar on his throat coupled with the healed broken nose and the slash along his cheekbone looked far worse.

Sweet finally asked, "Who hurt you, Bram?"

Bram swallowed for a hard pause because he didn't have to fucking pretend it was hard to talk about. "I just came off a rough job. Guys who screw insurance companies out of millions aren't fond of being caught." He spoke casually, knowing the haunted look in his eyes that met him daily in the mirror told a different story.

It was an easy sell. The truth always was, because no matter how couched, Bram couldn't hide the emotion that welled up when he discussed that "rough job."

Because *understatement of the year*.

And Sweet didn't seem to have a problem accepting what Bram told him. How long Bram could keep this ruse up was a different story.

It's all about finding Linc, making sure he's safe. And if Havoc could help him do that, hell, then Bram would pay the fucking bail money without issue.

Sweet unpacked the bag, passing the food to Bram. There was a small table with two chairs in the corner and both men sat, sharing the burgers and fries.

They ate in silence for a few moments, until Sweet asked, "So what made you pick that line of work?"

Bram's skill set wasn't always easy to hide, and an adjuster of high-level merchandise had to be part commando. Plus, there was no better time than the present to get in what would surely connect him to Havoc more than Linc. "After I left the military, I wanted to do something different."

"Sounds different," Sweet said, his voice neutral.

"Keeps me busy. Money's good and I get to travel, looking for precious artifacts," Bram lied.

"Army, right?"

"Just like Linc," Bram agreed, then ducked his head to hide his smile.

"What's that about?" Sweet asked.

Bram met his gaze. "I don't even have to ask—I can spot a Marine at twenty paces."

Sweet gave a short laugh. "I don't try to hide it."

"You couldn't." Bram reached over and grabbed some fries and realized it was the first time he recalled actually having an appetite versus shoving food down in order to gain back his energy. "This is good."

"Restaurant's around the corner. There's a bar there too. We'll head there later," Sweet promised.

"A Havoc bar?"

"Is that a problem?"

Bram shrugged. "Do most of them know Linc?"

"Everyone knows Linc. He made his mark in the short time he was here."

"That definitely sounds like my brother."

"It's a good thing, Bram. If anyone has any information, they'd have told me already. You're not the only one who's concerned."

So Sweet bringing him into this bar would be less like walking into the lion's den than Bram first thought.

At least that's what Bram told himself to keep from panicking.

But when Sweet stared at him like a predator at prey, Bram alternately wanted to bolt and strip.

Fuck. Fucking traitorous dick.

"I was thinking that letting you go last night was the stupidest thing I could've done," Sweet started, his drawl slow and sexy.

Bram, who'd spent the night half-hard himself thinking about Sweet, couldn't have agreed more. "Sometimes waiting pays off."

"It's definitely going to," Sweet murmured in a way that should've panicked him, but didn't.

"Look, I appreciate what you did for me . . ."

"Yeah?" Sweet sat back easily in his chair, spreading his legs. "You gonna make it up to me?"

Bram swallowed, his throat suddenly tight, his cock impossibly hard as Sweet motioned for him to come kneel between Sweet's legs. Bram supposed he could say no and be done with it, but hell, he hadn't wanted to say no last night and didn't want to tonight, either. So he slid to his knees, his face inches away from Sweet's jean-covered cock and yeah, he guessed he was.

This is a test, he reminded himself. MCs liked loyalty from everybody. He was playing a role. A game. One he at least got some pleasure from.

Sweet's hand carded through his hair, tugged a little to force Bram to look up at him. "Make no mistake, baby—this has nothing to do with what your brother owes Gypsy."

"You sure about that?" Bram asked. "You looked like you wanted to volunteer when Gypsy mentioned taking it out on my ass."

Sweet laughed, a deep rumble in his chest. "I wasn't about to let anyone else take that job on."

Bram smelled the leather, candy, and man combination that was distinctively Sweet. Without saying anything further, he worked the button and zipper on Sweet's jeans slowly, because Sweet hadn't worn underwear last night. Tonight was no different. Bram was up close and personal between Sweet's legs, and fuck, his cock was big and thick and hard—long enough to choke on.

He took his time, traced a vein on Sweet's shaft with his tongue as Sweet's hand remained in his hair, his legs spreading wider with every lick and lave. Bram tugged the man's jeans down farther so he could take his time exploring between his legs, driving Sweet crazy. Learning him.

Finally, when Sweet was growling, Bram took him inside his mouth and sucked hard, using his teeth to drag over the sensitive skin.

"Fuck yeah, that's it," Sweet groaned. Bram relaxed his throat to accept Sweet's thrusting into his mouth, fucking it to the rhythm Bram had set.

"If I tell you to do this in the middle of the bar tonight, you'll do it. Without question. Understood?" Sweet asked and Bram nodded, his mouth full of cock, lips stretched around him so Sweet could feel the hum of his satisfaction vibrate through his shaft and Christ, it was hard not to come just from Sweet's words. He wasn't kidding about it—Bram knew how it worked with MC members and their women. He guessed it wouldn't be any different for a gay member, but he'd never come across any.

He'd been ready to bring Sweet to climax, to swallow greedily, but Sweet had other plans. With a rough curse, he stood, pulling Bram off his dick and onto his feet.

He yanked at Bram's jeans, pushed them down as Bram kicked his shoes off. His T-shirt came off next and when he was completely naked, Sweet pushed him onto the bed on all fours.

Sweet kept his vest on and his jeans mostly on, and that was a turn-on for Bram, naked and helpless beneath the biker. Unable to move or think.

Sweet slapped his ass and Bram hissed, rocked his ass back as Sweet slid his cock in between Bram's ass cheeks, teasing him for several moments before pulling back and rubbing his lubed fingertips over Bram's hole and then working them inside of him. His head dropped and he groaned as Sweet hit his gland, rubbing it, making him squirm and yeah, he was going to come, and soon.

He felt Sweet's free hand gliding up his back and along the scars before dragging his palm back down over them, making the same motion several times like he was memorizing them. Before Bram got self-conscious about it, he heard the rip of a condom and with little fanfare, Sweet was inside of him.

Bram was good with that, because he came about two minutes after Sweet entered him. Sweet laughed, a glorious sound, and came right after. "I guess that's a compliment," he murmured, his scruff rough against Bram's cheek. "Next time, buckle up and prepare for more foreplay than you can handle."

Next time. Fuck. This had been a show of dominance. Bram comforted himself with the fact that Sweet no doubt just wanted the blowjob but couldn't keep his hands off Bram. It was a good sign in one way . . . and made him realize that in MC terms, he was halfway to being owned. That thought had him half collapsing onto his elbows and moaning into the pillow, aware that Sweet was laughing again as though reading his mind.

CHAPTER 4

OUT ON THE TILES

Bram showered quickly while Sweet waited downstairs in the shop. It allowed him to take his pain pills in private and also to grab his burner phone, his connection to Dozer. He figured it was safest to take that and leave his other cell in his bag.

He dragged on a tight, dark-gray thermal and black jean, then slid into black boots, the ones he'd used when he'd first learned to ride a bike. They were his lucky shoes, evidenced by the fact that he hadn't been killed the night he'd been wearing them.

Granted, the lucky part was mostly ironic—because it wasn't dumb luck but rather the Heathens MO. Heathens lived to torture their errant members. Their favorite mindfuck for traitors was what they called the Dead Man Walking: the traitor was beaten to the brink of death and left alive with the knowledge that they'd never stop looking for you. And they didn't, extending the beatings over a couple of years until you really did die. A lesson for all would-be Heathens to know that not only would you still bear the scars—internal and external—of what happened but you'd also walk around never knowing when or where the other shoe would drop.

Now, Bram shook off that memory as best he could, went and found Sweet, who was waiting at the bottom of the stairs.

"Ready?" Sweet asked, and Bram merely nodded and followed him out the door and into the big black truck parked out front. "The bar's only a couple of blocks away, but walking this time of night only asks for trouble."

Bram was surprised Sweet didn't have MC guards with him at all times and wondered how vulnerable both of them were at the moment. It was surprising. He'd learned, both from the ATF and more so from his insider access, just how much responsibility fell on the president of the MC. Sweet had all of Havoc on his shoulders and the fiscal responsibility alone could be staggering, never mind the juggling necessary to keep the prying eyes of the law away from the MC's illegal forays—and those that skated along the edge—and instead focus them on the more legitimate, if not illicit, businesses they ran. Keeping Sweet safe equaled keeping Havoc safe—they were one and the same.

Bram tried to think on what he'd really learned about Havoc through the Heathens, and realized it wasn't much. Havoc was legendary, spoken about in more reverent tones, which rarely happened in the Heathens MC.

Of course, some of the members didn't think Havoc would live up to the hype, but Bram had noted that none of them had ever wanted to try to prove it. While Havoc didn't have an angel's reputation as much as one of "we're too much trouble to fuck with"—since they helped as opposed to hurt the community—the law steered clear, as did most other MCs. Those who didn't learned quickly, or felt Havoc's wrath.

Bram heard firsthand accounts from Heathens, and they weren't pretty. While they weren't as completely deranged and vicious as Heathen kills, they were swift and merciless, and necessary. Havoc never retaliated directly against women or children, although they'd be the first to admit that those two groups would be affected if their men were killed.

Basics of surviving an MC? You didn't fuck with the MC, its members, their bikes, or their money.

"Can I ask about Linc at the bar?" That was, if any of the men actually talked to him.

Sweet maneuvered through the traffic-filled streets. "Let them bring it up first. Word travels fast—they'll know who you are."

"I'll bet," Bram muttered.

Sweet let that pass, asked instead, "When's the last time you heard from Linc, exactly?"

Bram met Sweet's gaze easily, because he was about to tell the truth. "Over a month ago. I was on the job so I couldn't check in much. When I ended up in the hospital, the docs tried to get in touch with him. He never called. And that's when I knew something was wrong, because that wasn't like him at all. But I couldn't do shit because I was out of it most of the time."

Sweet nodded as though something had been confirmed for him, and Bram added, "Linc never told you he had a brother, right?"

Sweet nodded. "You don't seem surprised."

"It was for protection. I tell Linc not to mention me. It's safer for both of us."

"I can see the evidence of why," Sweet said darkly.

"Comes a time when a guy needs to sit back and reassess," Bram admitted. Sweet stared at him but didn't say anything. "Granted, most men don't find themselves hanging out with a motorcycle gang while looking for their missing brother."

"Club, Bram, not a gang," Sweet told him automatically, as Bram caught sight of the bikes lined up diagonally along the length of the street outside the bar and the various other shops on the strip that were now closed, except for the tattoo parlor that was fully lit at the end of the block. Men in leather rockers spilled onto the sidewalks . . . and all of Bram's demons—both real and imagined—threatened to immediately rise up and revolt.

Sweet parked his truck in the alley next to the bar and looked over at Bram instead of getting out immediately. Tug and Ozzie, his two best enforcers, were under strict orders to stay five minutes behind. They'd wanted to follow him to the bar, but Sweet insisted on not freaking Bram out more than he already was. Hell, the only reason Sweet was in the damned cage and not on his own bike was because of Bram.

Bram, who looked around at the rows of bikes that lined the street outside the Havoc-owned bar, then shifted, visibly uncomfortable. "So no one here gives a shit you fuck men?"

"If they do, they know better than to say anything," Sweet told him. "I'm not the only gay guy here. Lots are straight, some bi. All that matters is that you're down for Havoc."

Bram's jaw tightened as Tug and Ozzie rode up behind them, bikes louder than hell. "Ride or die," he said hollowly.

"Something like that, yeah." He touched Bram's shoulder. "You're all right?"

"Fine," Bram lied, but Sweet didn't press him further. "Let's just go in."

Although Bram was still favoring his right side, Sweet knew that he was playing up the injury and nowhere near as helpless as he made himself appear. Now, Sweet moved his hand up and traced the white slice along Bram's cheek with his finger, Bram staring at him almost haughtily as he did so.

I need to figure him out—the man was law abiding enough to show up for Linc's bail . . . but he was also jumpy as fuck, no matter how hard he tried to hide it. Linc was no angel, but he'd been open about it. Sweet knew what he was getting with a guy like that when Linc had started hanging around Havoc, but Bram . . . well, Sweet supposed that's part of what kept him so damned intrigued despite his better sense. And if Bram hadn't been tense about going inside a biker bar, especially when the bikers were Havoc, it would've made Sweet suspicious. Didn't matter how trained men were. If they weren't a part of this club, they needed to be goddamned shitting in their pants when they came in, even though the only way to walk through these doors was with a Havoc member.

It was rare for Sweet to bring anyone in who wasn't from a neighboring Havoc-supported club. Okay, it never happened after Jimmy-Boy, so the stares he got weren't unexpected.

Bram was practically fucking rigid though.

"Come on, let's get some whiskey on board." Sweet urged him forward. Two seats cleared immediately at the bar, and he nodded at Bram to take one.

The mere fact that Bram had waited for Sweet's approval before doing so spoke volumes, to both Sweet and Havoc. It was noticed. It would be discussed.

It was in Bram's favor. Linc had shown the club respect from the start, but he'd been far more chill than the ball of stress currently sitting on the stool next to him.

Sweet had always been damned sure of himself, and he made sure he got what he wanted.

What he wanted right here and now was Bram. Simple as that.

The guy intrigued him. Turned him on. He didn't trust Bram, but he'd be stupid to. With the connection to Linc he'd be stupider still to not keep Bram close to Havoc, and to him. And Bram had to know that.

Sweet was aware of the fact that he had a soft heart toward military men who needed reintroduction to the world beyond the battlefield. That's what the MC had been built on, but with Jimmy-Boy it'd blown up for him on a personal level. He'd been lucky it hadn't affected the MC's businesses or safety, and that was only because he'd sworn—to himself and to Havoc—that the MC came first.

And it always would.

The bar was crowded, a mix of several different MCs. Bram saw Havoc's rocker a lot, Hangmen MC and a few Kill Devils. Obviously, the clubs were on relatively good terms with one another, evidenced here by the current lack of bloodshed.

He nursed his longneck and listened to the blisteringly loud rock blasting through the speakers. There were some MC old ladies here—a few bartenders and servers and the others? Women who came in looking for a thrill. Or a scare. Or a combination of both.

That part reminded him of the Heathens clubhouse. Heat. Sex. The bar wasn't nearly as private as a clubhouse, but to Bram it seemed like this was where people Havoc wanted to fuck were vetted.

He had a feeling most conquests never made it past this bar. He wasn't sure if he wanted to be one of the lucky few, but that was because he knew more than most.

Of course, being a part of the Heathens started off okay. Brotherhood and shit. Family they'd never had. Money. Freedom. And then it got dark and by then, for most, it was too late. He'd known how bad those guys were going in and he'd still gotten caught up in it at first. It was like a drug, especially if you grew up with no adults to depend on.

Clubs like Havoc didn't take many recruits, so most men looking to get involved in a MC were left with the bottom-of-the-barrel clubs like the Heathens. That wasn't so much Havoc's fault as it was the way of the world.

Block the good way, they'll find the bad.

As the music got louder, Bram tried unsuccessfully not to get drunk, but his old friends Paranoia and PTSD did a tango. He was more worried about giving himself away than being drunk and remained next to Sweet as men and women came up to him, one after the other, shaking his hand, coming in for a hug or just generally wanting a word with the president of Havoc.

Bram accepted his role of the standby because, bottom line, he wasn't finding Linc tonight. Tonight was just another night in a long line of Bram fighting for his life and so, when one of Sweet's hands went behind his neck, Bram was already ramped up.

"Hey, relax," Sweet told him.

Yeah, right. "Trying to."

"I'm just going to talk to one of our fellow MC reps." Sweet jerked his head toward the far corner of the bar. "You'll be all right?"

"I'm not a fucking child," Bram growled.

Sweet smiled. "Trust me—know that."

Bram watched him walk away, then turned back toward the bar where the TV was on—some stupid sitcom, but Bram figured staring at that was better than staring at the crowd and having it be misinterpreted.

A beer bottle shattered, cutting through the loudness. For a moment the bar went silent as every man assessed for danger and most seemed to immediately process *accident* . . . except for Bram, who blinked and saw the scene from months ago as clearly as ever.

A Heathen breaking his beer bottle over an innocent college kid's head. The kid's stunned look.

Another bottle breaking over his head. And another and another and then the kid was on the floor, his skull split, his face unrecognizable, bloodied and broken, a soft moan breaking through the now-inhuman-like face—

"You're with Sweet?" one of the Havoc men asked, and Bram jerked his head toward the biker's direction, forcing himself to erase any signs of panic.

"Yeah—I'm Bram." He gulped his beer to try to erase the taste, the smell of blood that wafted through his senses whenever he thought of the college kid's beatdown.

"You looking to patch in?"

"No," Bram said truthfully.

The biker looked him up and down, no doubt taking in Bram's build, the tattoos, the stance. "Military?"

"Army."

"Pussies in the Army."

"Guess we learned it from the jarheads," Bram said easily, sliding back into the military banter that he recalled so well. That was another brotherhood, with a camaraderie that he often missed.

Granted, he was playing with a bit of fire here. He wasn't part of this brotherhood of bikers, but the military bond would typically transcend that if he stuck to military insults and kept the MC out of it.

Tonight, it thankfully did. It probably helped that he was fucking the president of the MC too but . . .

"Fucking Army," the biker said with a hard shake of his head as a second biker rounded in on Bram's other side and leaned an elbow on the bar next to Bram, boxing him in. "Need another beer?"

"Let me get you one." Bram turned and motioned to the bartender. "A round for these guys on my tab, okay?" He handed them the longneck bottles a second later.

"So, when'd you get out?" the first biker asked. "I'm Mac, by the way."

"Bram. Been out for a while now."

The second gave him a rough pat on the shoulder. "I'm Tug. You're Linc's brother, right?"

"Guilty as charged. I've been looking for him."

"Not the only one," Tug said cryptically, and Bram figured he was talking about Gypsy but wasn't willing to push it.

And then Sweet was back and Tug and Mac were gone. "They say anything about Linc?"

"Not much." Bram paused. "Are they cool with me because I'm Army, or because of you?"

Sweet laughed. "They're just testing you. They might seem nice, but that's because they're not going to put energy into fucking with you if they don't know if you're sticking around."

Bram figured that was the truth. They saw him as disposable so no reason to waste energy hating him.

Somehow, that made him feel like shit. Which made him realize how completely fucked up he actually was. *It's not like you want their acceptance, dumbass.*

Then again . . .

Sweet broke into his thoughts. "You've got that look on again."

"What? No, I'm just tired."

Sweet seemed like he didn't quite believe him, but then Tug called, "Pagans outside, boss. Asking for you by name."

Sweet's demeanor went from casual to Satan in three seconds flat. Anger radiated off him as he stood, all MC business. "I'll take care of them."

"Sweet," Tug started but Sweet flashed him a look and Tug put his hands up and took a step back.

Interesting. Sweet fought his own battles—literally—and his men were ready and willing to not only back him up but take on the fight for their president, which spoke volumes about Havoc.

Part of Bram wanted to see Sweet fight. Needed to. The law enforcement part of him reminded him that out of sight, out of mind was probably the best way to go here. He couldn't report what he couldn't see, couldn't get in trouble for not reporting what didn't happen in front of him.

But since Bram and law enforcement weren't exactly seeing eye to eye these days, he followed Sweet as he strode through the bar and the crowds seemed to break apart ahead of him. He definitely had the commanding-presence thing down pat, but it wasn't an act. Sweet had the charismatic personality Bram associated with leaders.

It made Bram trust him both more and less, because he'd never had a great track record with authority figures. But he still watched from the sidewalk as Sweet went right toward the three Pagan MC members who hung in the middle of the street. Bram noted that both took a step back as Sweet approached before realizing they looked like pussies and held their ground.

He couldn't hear what Sweet was saying, but the Pagans clearly weren't happy about it. One of them reached back to swing, but Sweet caught the man's fist and twisted his arm behind his back, taking the first Pagan to the ground.

The second stepped in and tried to take Sweet down. Got an elbow to the nose for his troubles and reeled back, howling in pain as blood sprayed everywhere. Sweet let go of the first guy's arm, grabbed the second by the hair and smashed the Pagan's face into his knee before lifting his head back up to whisper in his ear.

Bram was caught up in forcing himself to stand still.

Don't get involved. You'll bring scrutiny you can't afford onto you.

But the damned flash of the blade—no one else saw what he'd been trained to. These men had instincts and they could fight, but there was something to be said for being scared enough to fight for your life, which put his situational awareness through the damned roof.

He moved forward, sliding easily past Tug and sneaking up on all of them, including Sweet. Before Sweet—or the Pagans—could react, Bram had the man with the knife in his hand and was dragging the guy's arm behind his back, forcing the knife to drop. He kicked it away, slammed the guy's face to the ground and held him there, boot to neck, and Sweet took on the unarmed Pagans.

That was a sight to see. Bram had no doubt Sweet could've handled himself against all of them, hand-to-hand. But the knife was a deal breaker . . . and the man under Bram's foot had every intention of using it. So he stood there, waiting until the fight was over and the Pagans were reeling, until the police sirens whooped, too close for comfort, and Sweet jerked his head toward Bram. "Go inside. Now."

Bram did—couldn't afford an arrest, because then Parisi would be notified. He walked away and Tug closed the door of the bar behind him.

"What'll happen?" Bram asked, even though he knew they'd all be brought in and none of them would talk.

"Police will take them. Question and release, but not till morning," Tug said gruffly. "You'll have to come with us."

"Me? Why? I'm staying at Gypsy's place," Bram said.

"Not now. Sweet wouldn't want you unprotected—not after this. We'll grab your stuff and head there." Tug's tone left no room for argument.

And Gypsy? He was right there agreeing, saying, "I have to be on call for Sweet in case there's a miracle bail request. But Havoc's on lockdown, which means the bond shop's number forwards to my house. Go with Ozzie and wait at the back for me."

Ozzie's head was half-shaved, a longer piece left in a mohawk strip that was tied up at the back of his head. He wore a Havoc rocker, dark stubble, and a hoop in each ear and still somehow looked like the most masculine son of a bitch. His hands fisted, tattoos marking the lower knuckle of each finger, spelling out his MC's name, and his eyes had sparked fire as he watched the Pagans waiting for Sweet.

Ozzie had a hand on his shoulder, guiding him toward the back of the bar. The crowd had resumed partying as if nothing had happened, the music blared, every person in the room willing to provide alibis. Even so, all the MC men were tense, poised to strike if needed.

Bram was exactly the same way—born, bred, and ready to fight his way out of everything. He waited with Ozzie at the back and finally forced himself to asked, "Will the Pagans report him?" even though he knew that'd never happen.

Still, he had to keep up his cover as Linc's dumb-as-fuck brother.

Ozzie snorted. "Never. Cops just decide to scoop everyone up and hope someone talks. It's more about the Pagans than Havoc, but we're used to it."

Bram wondered what the fuck he was supposed to do. "Gypsy made it sound like bail wasn't an option."

"They'll just let him out in the morning. Nothing to charge him with," Ozzie explained. "Sweet's okay."

The familiar swirl of emotions began inside his brain. Locked up, unprotected. *Sweet isn't you*, he reminded himself.

Minutes later, he was in Sweet's truck with Tug driving, Gypsy in the passenger's seat and Bram and Ozzie behind them. When they got to the bond shop, the men worked with military precision: Tug waited in the car, Ozzie took the front door, and Gypsy vetted the entire building before he told Bram, "Go get your shit and come down fast."

Bram did so. His bag was still packed, save for the shirt he'd changed from earlier. He grabbed it from the bathroom and stared at his face in the mirror, the hunted, haunted expression staring back at him.

What the hell had he been thinking? Two nights of cock—damned good cock, but still, it wasn't a reason for him to run around saving a biker.

Shit. He splashed his face with cold water, rubbed it hard with a towel. He'd be sleeping—if that happened—fully clothed and armed. Then he grabbed his bag and got back into the truck that would take him into the Havoc MC compound.

CHAPTER 5

JAILBREAK

Bram wasn't sure if he was prisoner or protected, and driving into Havoc with the lights on the truck dimmed didn't do anything to reassure him it wasn't the former. He took note of several MC guards at what he assumed was the entrance, but from there, it was dark as shit on the property, at least until Tug turned up a small road and came upon a lighted house that Bram assumed was Gypsy's.

"Wait here," Gypsy told him and went with Tug into the house. Several minutes later, Ozzie's phone beeped and he walked Bram into the custom-made log cabin that looked nothing like the shitholes that most of the Heathens inhabited.

Ozzie walked him into the kitchen where Gypsy and Tug stood talking. Gypsy handed him a bottle of water. "I'm going to let these guys out and lock up. There'll be guys around the house all night."

Was that a warning? Bram just nodded as the three men walked past him. But before he could think more on that, he noticed the shirt hanging casually on the back of one of Gypsy's kitchen chairs. There was no way this wasn't a setup, a motherfucking trap set because they didn't believe he was Linc's brother, like Bram was some kind of jerk-off.

His hands tightened into fists, but the instinct to reach for Linc's shirt was stronger. As he held it, he was immediately flooded with memories.

It was a concert T-shirt for Motörhead, the first concert they'd gone to together. Linc loved the shirt, said the goddamned thing was indestructible. Faded from black to grayish with age, frayed, the cotton nearly see-through in places. It was Linc's security blanket.

It went overseas with him, and Bram was pretty sure Linc regarded it like some kind of talisman.

Tonight, Bram would clutch it like one, although it wouldn't stop the dreams.

He didn't wait for Gypsy to come back into the kitchen, figured that the shirt had been left there to goad Bram into a reaction—or to see if he actually recognized it at all. So he took the shirt, because that should clue the asshole in to the fact that Bram knew exactly whose shirt it was. He also grabbed a couple of beers and a bottle of water for good measure and found the room his bag had been placed in. He remained dressed, downed the beers in quick succession and lay down, and he'd locked the damned door and slept with his knife.

Gypsy didn't come to find him, remained outside with Tug and Ozzie for quite a while before Bram heard the door open and close. But there were Havoc members at all the exits of the house, just like Gypsy told him there would be. Whether they were to keep him safe or a prisoner, Bram had no idea. Probably a little of both.

Fuck, he was really isolated. Except for Dozer, no one knew where he was. He especially couldn't tell Linnea his location—he needed her and her kids, his nephews, safe.

But he also needed to check-in, so he used his burner to call her as he did a quick sweep for bugs and cameras, found nothing but turned the TV on anyway. "Hey Lin—"

"Where have you been? I've left messages," she cut him off. "And don't pull that job shit."

Yeah, he couldn't get away with anything with her. Neither could Linc. "Sorry. I was following a lead on Linc and getting settled."

"You still haven't heard from him? What did the bondsman say?"

"That Linc jumped." He considered telling her that Linc might not have left on his own steam, but why go there?

And still, their sister was anything but stupid. "I want to believe he ran, because thinking anything else . . ."

After she trailed off, all he could say was, "I know, Lin. I know."

"Find our baby brother."

Our baby brother. There were no *halves* or *steps* with Linnea—her brothers were hers. They were family, period. "I will, Lin. Promise." He paused. "How're the boys?"

"Pains in the asses, just like my brothers." Then her tone softened. "They miss their uncles."

"Tell them we'll see them soon. I mean it."

"I know. Stay safe or I'll kill you."

He hung up, knowing she meant that. She'd known the full extent of his injuries, but only after the fact. It was better that way, but he'd hear about it for the rest of his life.

He took up Linc's concert shirt and held it, like it could tell him where his brother was. He concentrated hard, recalling all the times he'd seen Linc in that shirt, and happy. Linc always looked more like an angel, Linnea used to say, albeit a fallen one with a very crooked halo and a smile that could make anyone forgive him. Blond, blue eyes, their mom's olive skin that tanned well and an easy, lanky build he wore like a strutting model.

A hippie, trained to kill. It was a great cover, but that was exactly who Linc was—he knew it, embraced it, enjoyed the fuck out of it. Unlike Bram, who could never just keep one life or persona on for size. There were too many he wanted to try, looking for the perfect hit. One that felt comfortable without being too restrictive.

But no matter how well he looked out for Linc, Bram could never shake the feeling that it really was the other way around. And still he refused to believe or accept that his baby brother was the one babying him, just kept insisting that he knew best and Linc would nod—patiently—and then do whatever the fuck he wanted to keep himself happy, which often included asking Bram what he planned on doing post-ATF.

"There is no post-ATF, Linc. This is my job," he'd say, and Linc would nod, stare at him with that combination of spacey and sage, and then ask, "You don't think there's more out there for you?"

"More? More what?"

"More . . . life," Linc would say, spreading his arms to emphasize his point.

Fuck it all. The only thing Bram knew for sure was that he wanted what was best for Linc.

Bram took out a pain pill and contemplated taking it. He'd rather keep drinking to numb out everything, but it hadn't helped the physical pain much. He had to weigh the worst of the two and finally, he took the damned pill, let himself float away from everything, good and bad. And still, it did nothing to quell his nightmares, his dreams a mix of Linc and the beating and pure fucking terror.

He woke yelling, clutching Linc's shirt.

Sweet remained locked up for the rest of the night through early the next day. He'd been solitary in his cell, mostly left alone except for the guard who'd smuggled him a bag of lollipops, and finally questioned half-heartedly by the detective who had to answer to the FBI who roamed the area looking for RICO cases.

"Nothing personal, Sweet," Detective Connelly told him as he sat across the interrogation table.

Whenever they got to this point in his arrest, Sweet knew he was just about to be let go for lack of evidence. The understanding between Havoc and the local law had always been an uneasy partnership, but most of the cops understood that Havoc was a necessary evil to keep the drugs and guns and gangs away from their city.

Havoc also stimulated the local economy with the shops they ran off the Havoc compound, which also helped keep the local politicians from coming down too hard on them.

One of Havoc's biggest moneymakers was porn, which was filmed, cut, and distributed on Havoc's property—completely legal and up to code. Taxes paid. Another was stealing expensive cars from wealthy buyers. "I know. Too bad I didn't see anything."

Connelly stared at Sweet's bloodied knuckles and shook his head. "A damned shame."

Now, nearly twelve hours post-arrest, with Tug and Ozzie escorting him home, Sweet dialed Gypsy.

"They finally got tired of you?" Gypsy asked.

"About fuckin' time." He needed a shower, sex, and sleep, in that order. "Bram okay?"

"Apart from the nightmares?"

"How bad?"

"Bad, Sweet. But he made Linc's shirt. I left it out purposely."

Sweet's anger rose but he wasn't sure exactly why—it was a smart move on Gypsy's part. "So he passed your test."

"Go fuck yourself, Sweet," Gypsy muttered. "Come get Bram and get him the hell out."

Gypsy was the only man on this compound who'd talk to Sweet that way. Their fights didn't last long though, and Sweet always cut his friend slack.

"What the hell's got you so spooked?"

"How about the fact that this guy's got you wrapped," Gypsy told him.

"Guess it runs in the family," Sweet retorted and swore he could hear Gypsy's growl through the phone. "Hey, I trusted you about Linc."

"And look where that got us."

"Maybe. Maybe not."

"Bram's fucked up, Sweet. We both know it. Just because you're looking for someone to save . . ." Gypsy trailed off as Sweet's blood ran cold.

He stared out the window and hung up on Gypsy before he said something he'd regret, figured his friend was more pissed—and guilt ridden—over Linc than anything at the moment, and Sweet's choices were an easy target.

But Gypsy was dead wrong about Sweet wanting to save anyone. He'd learned long ago that it wasn't possible, and he lived daily with regrets over things he could never take back. But he'd learned from what happened with James, aka Jimmy-Boy, and after losing the love of his goddamned life, Sweet refused to make the same mistake twice.

Still, he pondered on the value of keeping Bram on the compound until they could figure out what the fuck was happening. Because Sweet had administered a test of his own, one his closest MC brothers definitely noticed. By Sweet's pretending not to see the knife, he'd forced Bram's hand to see if he'd jump into the fight . . . and ultimately, it'd forced Bram farther into Havoc. It was done to ensure that Linc would come back, or to at least find out once and for all if Linc had betrayed Havoc. And if Bram was planning on doing the same.

This plan would screw Bram with the Pagans, and it might end up doing the same to Sweet. But he'd risk it to ferret out any signs of infiltration from outside enemies into his camp. Havoc trusted him implicitly. They depended on him. He'd never let his club down.

CHAPTER 6

I'M GONNA CRAWL

After his nightmare, Bram wouldn't let himself go back to sleep. He'd been sitting on the edge of the bed in Gypsy's spare room since 4 a.m., staring out the window watching darkness turn to light like a prisoner waiting for release.

He'd eaten a few protein bars he'd had stashed in his bag so he could take some more pain pills, because he'd noticed his hands shook if he didn't dose up. They'd stopped making him feel so groggy, and whether that was a good or bad sign he wasn't sure, but he was sure as hell he needed to be pain-free physically to deal with Havoc. To defend himself and find Linc in the process, because this time he needed Linc's help. Maybe he was living it up partying while hiding from Havoc and responsibility, and Bram would accept that as long as he could get Linc back. Because fuck, he missed the hell out of his brother.

Gypsy hadn't gotten much sleep either—Bram heard him pacing around the house, talking on the phone and finally heard the door slam. A quick glance out the window assured him that Gypsy was now outside with the men who'd been guarding the house all night. Bram turned the TV up and took the opportunity to check in with Dozer. It was under the twelve-hour mark, but who the hell knew when the next opportunity would present itself?

"Where are you?" Dozer asked immediately in lieu of hello.

Bram checked the window again—Gypsy and the two MC guards remained in a tight circle, their heads together. "Havoc. Gypsy's house. Sweet got arrested."

"Are you trying to kill yourself?" Dozer hissed. "Because I'll come get you and check you in someplace until you're motherfucking semi-sane."

The hairs on the back of Bram's neck rose. "Hear anything?"

"You're definitely on the Heathens' radar. Big time."

"Do they know—"

"That you're not who you say you are?" Dozer finished his thought. "Not yet. But someone is leaking intel about where your undercover persona is at the moment."

Bram had never been more grateful than now that he was a paranoid bastard. Because the only person he'd told his made-up vacation plans to was Parisi, and Bram had mentioned that he'd be on the other side of the country. "And?"

"It's California."

Bram's gut feeling about Parisi was confirmed as he breathed, "Okay then."

"What's your end game?"

Bram sighed. "Safety."

"For a few minutes and the cost is high. What're you going to pay with?"

Bram had no idea how to answer that. "Look, I need to figure out more about where Linc could've gone. There's a missing piece and it's here, at Havoc."

"So find Linc, pay the bond, and get the fuck out."

Yes, that was the best option. The rest of it, whether he was betrayed to the Heathens or whether he ended up going back to the ATF? All up in the air. "Don't let yourself get fucked for me, Doz."

"You're not the boss of me," Dozer warned before hanging up. Their familiar refrain made Bram smile for a second, until he remembered that Parisi was trying to let the Heathens kill him.

He shoved Linc's T-shirt into his bag, zipped it up and went into the kitchen to wait for Gypsy. What he needed now was a current address for Linc. His brother did mainly e-billing these days, and any addresses still listed were his previous rentals. Linc had mentioned that he'd been spending time at Havoc, but living here?

If Gypsy was surprised to see him waiting in the kitchen, packed bag and all, he didn't show it. Instead, he asked, "Hungry?"

"Any word on Sweet?" Bram countered.

"Nope. Why? Got somewhere to be?"

"I'd like to go to Linc's place and check it out."

"You didn't do that first, before you came to me?" Gypsy asked.

"I don't have a current address. But you do."

Gypsy shrugged. "He was staying with Rush for a while but then Rush mainly stays here."

Fuck. "Where's Rush's place?" he demanded, and when Gypsy didn't answer, he added, "I guess you went there and looked around."

"His bike's gone, Bram. He's a runner. Rush said so, you said so, and hell, even Linc said so. The landlord hasn't seen him, but Linc paid rent through the end of this month."

"And that's it?"

"You're a month behind," Gypsy told him.

"So what the fuck've *you* been doing besides making calls to me?" Bram asked, and Gypsy's eyes turned into cold steel. Bram could feel the warning signs radiating off the man, but he didn't give a shit. "This is your goddamned job, so why not find him right away? Or do you always fuck your money and then let it walk?"

"This wasn't about money," Gypsy said tightly.

"Then what the fuck was it about?" Bram railed, as it finally clicked that Linc saying he loved it at Havoc translated to Linc loving Gypsy. And all Bram's anger that had previously been directed at Linc shot straight at Gypsy. The fucker had taken his brother's heart and stomped it, had let him down and let him go. At the very least, he'd done shit to look for him, focusing on the lost money aspect ahead of anything else. "You've let my brother's trail go stone-cold. All I've seen you do is dial my goddamned number. So either you suck at your business so badly you can't even find your own dick with a map—"

Gypsy charged, a bull seeing red, and it was exactly what Bram needed. He'd feel it in the places that were still healing, but in the heat of this moment, he didn't care. Maybe they'd kick him out of Havoc—and it was definitely easier fighting one man to do that than the whole club.

Gypsy was strong, seemed as angry as Bram. Both men took it out on each other, Bram's fist connecting with Gypsy's nose, Gypsy's landing squarely against Bram's sternum, vibrating through his still healing and painful as fuck rib cage.

As Bram fought for breath, Gypsy growled, "Don't blame me because you can't take care of your own."

"He was yours too, you fucker." Bram rallied, managed to get Gypsy in a headlock, ready to slam his knee into Gypsy's nose. Just then Sweet grabbed him with a loud, "What the fuck?" as he yanked Bram's arms off Gypsy and behind his back, leaving him effectively wide open to Gypsy's blows.

Bram fought the hold, not wanting to give away how well he could fight, but thankfully Gypsy backed off, swearing, blood pouring from his nose. Bram's head had opened over his eyebrow. Those bled like a bitch but he was too wound up on adrenaline to feel the punishing pain he was assured of later.

Finally, Sweet managed to drag Bram outside the house. When they got several feet away from the front door, Sweet let him go with a hard shove. "Calm the fuck down, Bram."

Bram turned, not liking the threat in Sweet's tone. "Or what?"

He moved toward Sweet, but Ozzie and Tug were coming up on him. Sweet put a hand up and then grabbed Bram again, yanking his arm up behind his back, not hard, but enough to immobilize. "Breathe and rethink this."

"Nothing to rethink. He's done shit about looking for Linc and it's my fault?"

"He's your brother," Gypsy yelled as he stood in the open front door.

"And he's just a fuck to you, right?" Bram shot back. "He probably fucking loved you and you threw him away."

Gypsy flinched, like he'd been hit by a physical blow.

"Gypsy, just move away," Sweet told him in a tone that brokered no nonsense.

"What do you want from me, Sweet? I'll fucking pay. All I want to do is find my brother, and you're putting up roadblocks." Bram wrenched away from him. "Why? What do all you have against him?"

"Nothing. But you need to calm the fuck down."

"I need to calm down? Fuck that—he was taunting me," Bram growled, and Sweet didn't bother to deny it. "Testing me when my flesh and blood is out there, maybe twisting in the wind, and Gypsy's sitting with his thumb in his ass nursing his poor broken heart like a bitch."

At his words, Gypsy broke something inside his house that crashed with a resounding shatter.

"I want to go to Linc's place. Getting his address was like pulling motherfucking teeth," he said, hearing the obvious frustration in his own voice.

"Gypsy would never let you leave Havoc on your own—and without my permission. That's the way it goes, for your own protection. You jumped in with me on the Pagans. You'll be rewarded for that on their end, and you won't like it one fucking bit," Sweet warned.

"I appreciate the protection but—"

"You should appreciate it," Sweet told him.

Bram shook his head. "Sweet—"

"I'll take you tomorrow."

"I'm wasting time—it needs to be today. Now," Bram bit out, knowing he'd pushed it too goddamned far.

He also didn't care.

"Get in the car," Sweet growled. "Or I swear to fuck I'll tie you up and throw you in."

He would, too. Bram had no doubt about that. He glanced around, took in Tug and Ozzie, and knew he could take them on and out, but fuck, he wasn't happy about it. He slammed into the truck as Sweet got into the driver's side and shot away from Gypsy's house. Tug and Ozzie stayed behind, but Sweet was taking him deep into what Bram assumed was still Havoc country. It was isolated out here, and although it was a sunny afternoon, the trees were thick, shading the area . . . and Bram was wound up as anything and still feeling the pain.

"Grab some gauze out of the glove compartment. You're bleeding like hell," was all Sweet said on the drive. Bram did, pressed the gauze tight to the cut on his eyebrow and realized he couldn't erase the possibility that Havoc had something to do with Linc's disappearance. They were an MC, not Boy Scouts, and Bram had seen a lot of fucked-up things "family" did to one another in the name of wanting to help.

When Sweet finally pulled over and got out, Bram did too, in a self-defense stance more than anything. When Sweet moved close, Bram slammed his palm against Sweet's chest to keep him from coming closer.

Bram's gut clenched. "If you're trying to scare me, know I don't scare easy."

"Think I don't know that?" Sweet demanded. "You're a danger to yourself. You want to find Linc, right? That's your ultimate goal?"

Bram hung his head and breathed. Finally, he met Sweet's eyes. "Did you bring me up here to kill me if I didn't agree with you?"

"I brought you up here to fuck you without being bothered. Been thinking about fucking you since last night," Sweet growled. "Even more today. You make me want to fuck that fight right out of you."

Bram's breath caught, because it was the opposite of what he'd assumed would happen here, but he couldn't help the sarcasm that came out of his mouth next. "Want me to blow you as payment in return for taking me to Linc's? Or for the protection?"

Sweet watched him like he was prey. "I was ready to throw you on the back of my bike and fuck you after the fight. It's all I thought about in jail."

"So you take me to the woods, huh?" He didn't even rate a back room at Havoc's bar, but hell, he was horny. Angry. He had to work it all out somehow. Had to get Sweet to his happy place before he fully remembered that Bram had been ready to beat the shit out of a Havoc member.

Sweet smirked. "This is Havoc land. I realize you don't get where you are—or what it means that you've been brought here for protection, but I enjoy a challenge, so keep going."

Bram did. "For all I know, you made Linc disappear. Any graves around here I should be looking for?"

"Bram—"

"Did you plant evidence on him so you could set him up and kill him? Because you fucking set me up with that knife shit last night."

Sweet didn't deny it. "But you still jumped in."

"Yeah. I don't like seeing three against one." There it was again, the hollow-voiced tone that came out whenever Bram discussed anything MC-related. "Can you just fucking take me to Linc's?"

Part request and part demand, but something in Bram's tone must've clutched at Sweet's heart. "Yeah, Bram, we can go now."

CHAPTER 7

HOW MANY MORE TIMES

As Sweet drove him to Linc's place, Bram asked, "Have you spoken to the landlord or are we going to go there and break in?" with an extra dose of sarcasm, still pissed about having to be chauffeured around with a bodyguard.

"His name's Tony and he lives close enough," Sweet started, with a patience Bram didn't understand. "I just texted him to meet us there. I told him I was bringing Linc's brother to check mail. He definitely paid three months in advance—and he's got three weeks left."

"Yeah—Gypsy told me," Bram said tightly.

"Your brother jumped bond. You said yourself, he's got a rep for running."

Bram stared out the window, unwilling to let the club—or himself—off the hook. "I want to check it out but leave the place intact . . . for when he gets back."

Sweet wisely just nodded and the rest of the drive was quiet, save for Sweet's radio playing a mix of old-school rock and Grateful Dead tunes.

Twenty minutes later they pulled in front of a small house on a suburban-looking street, a decidedly un-Linc place. Bram exited the truck and was walking toward the man who'd been sitting on the front steps. "Tony? I'm Bram—Linc's brother."

Sweet was right behind him, and Tony shook both their hands. If he knew what Sweet's rocker meant, he didn't seem to have an issue with it. "Hey, is Linc okay? I haven't seen him around. He's paid up and all, but I was just wondering. It didn't seem like him to pick up and leave."

Apparently, Shades was some kind of Stepford town that made everyone act in the exact opposite manner they normally did.

And Bram decided to go with the truth here. "Actually, I was hoping to find some information inside his place. We haven't heard from him in a while either."

"Oh man." Tony looked upset.

"I'm sure he's fine. Linc's a free spirit. Sometimes he takes off on trips and forgets to tell people," Bram tried to reassure him, but Tony still appeared worried.

"Keep those keys, okay? I've got another set—like I said, rent's paid, and you're his brother, so if you're planning on crashing here, go for it. And let me know if you want to keep paying—I'm cool with renting to you."

Next to him, Sweet tensed slightly. Bram felt an instant relief at actually having an escape if necessary. "That's great. Thanks. I'll be hanging around Shades for a while."

"Can you call me when you hear from him?" Tony asked.

"Absolutely," Bram assured him, and then Tony left and Bram and Sweet headed up to the rental house.

The mail slot was cut into the front door, which meant they had to push aside a month's worth of mail to get inside.

"Cell phone bill." Sweet pointed to a Verizon bill on top of the pile.

"Already tried the GPS. It's off." Bram glanced around. The place was small—clean but still dusty from being locked up for a while. Linc always kept his spaces clean and slightly disheveled.

Bram wandered the house, feeling like he was invading his brother's privacy. Linc had no real boundaries about that, though—Bram was definitely projecting.

It didn't look like Linc had been taken from here by force, but it also didn't look like he'd had any plans to leave. Nothing was even partially packed. There were empty suitcases in the closet. He went through Linc's clothes, then found a lock box that he picked and found a passport and other important papers. He'd take that with him.

He also found a bong. Baggie of weed, books, movies. Old food in the fridge. No cell phone or wallet or bike. Bram knew realistically that if Linc had run, the fact that he'd left so much behind really wasn't all that surprising. Linc had the ways and means to become someone else—he didn't need much but himself but he'd become attached to Shades. And Havoc. And Gypsy.

None of it made sense.

While Bram sat on the floor and attacked the mail pile quietly, Sweet cleaned out the fridge and took the garbage outside. By the time he returned, Bram was numb. The envelopes were mostly junk mixed with a few real bills but nothing to give Bram any clue as to where his brother had disappeared to—or why.

"Has he done this before?" Sweet asked finally.

Bram glanced up at him. "Sure. When he went into Basic, he didn't tell anyone. Skipped out like this. But since then . . . with Rush and Noah . . ."

Rush and Noah—Linc's best friends and constant companions in troublemaking. They seemed to keep each other on somewhat of an even keel, which Bram was grateful for. Last Bram heard, Rush was hooked up with an XO from Havoc and Noah was hanging out with the Hangmen MC and dating the president's daughter.

"Rush's been away for a couple of months," Sweet explained. "Noah too."

Bram glanced around and saw a few envelopes that had slid partially under the front mat. One of them was a bank statement, and Bram cursed himself that he hadn't thought to check up on this before. He scanned it quickly, noted that zero money had moved except for bills set to auto-pay. And a gas station fill up on . . .

Wait. He showed Sweet the date. "Ring a bell?"

"I can't be sure, but that's within the week he disappeared," Sweet agreed.

"Can we narrow it down?"

"I'll ask Gypsy."

"Right," Bram bit out, and for maybe the first time during all of this, his thoughts skittered briefly where he'd fought so hard to not let them—that there was a very goddamned real possibility Linc was in real trouble. Because his brother had never run and left the equivalent of his entire life behind without cleaning up purposefully after himself. *Never.* And once Bram let that thought break down the door, the possibility of foul play and Linc hurt—or worse—flooded through and threatened to drown him.

"No," he said out loud. "No. No. No." And he repeated it until the other thoughts receded and he was able to convince himself to believe Linc was alive. Maybe in a bit of trouble, like always or maybe living a whole new life and enjoying the fuck out of himself.

But Bram pulled his knees up to his chest and rocked, despite the physical pain it caused him. The emotional pain overrode everything else.

He was aware that Sweet was talking him through the panic attack, gently helping him uncurl. After God knew how long, Bram sat, useless, staring out the window, wondering how the hell everything had gotten so fucked.

Finally, he looked Sweet in the eye and admitted, "I was mad at Linc. So goddamned mad that I had to come and deal with the trouble he'd gotten himself into. I never thought . . . if I'd bothered to keep up more, maybe . . ."

"Stop," Sweet ordered. "None of us thought to worry."

"I'm his brother. I'm supposed to protect him," Bram said fiercely.

"Get yourself together. We'll find him."

"Why are you doing this, Sweet?" he asked suddenly, the roar between his ears threatening to become a deafening tsunami that would attack anyone and everyone in his path, deserved or not.

"Linc's been good to Rush. Rush is one of ours," Sweet said simply. "And Gypsy."

"Right." Linc snorted. "Look, I'm fucked up, Sweet. It's not something I can exactly hide being in such close proximity, but make no mistake, I'll go to the ends of the earth for my family."

"Who fucked you up? Tell me who—and why they did it." It was a gentle demand, coaxing, and Bram almost caved.

Instead, he closed his eyes. "I don't want to talk about it."

"Why not?"

"Because I should be motherfucking dead," he practically shouted.

Sweet looked pained, and unsurprised. "I need to know everything."

"And I need to get the fuck out of here. Why won't you let me go?"

"Because you're a fucking danger to yourself right now. You're in pain and you need to detox from pain meds. You're drinking too much."

Bram shook his head. "None of this is your concern. Take this." He offered Sweet the money order he'd been keeping in his pocket. "And I'm out."

"I'm not taking it."

"Why? So I'll owe you?"

Sweet's hand slid to Bram's neck, half cupping, half holding him in a submissive pose. "Yeah, you owe me. I owe you too. So let me owe you, dammit."

"What else do you want? My ass? Is that on the line too, or are you just going to share it with random people who work at your bars?"

Sweet flinched. "You didn't seem to mind it."

"And I guess you're always right. No one's going to go against you. Guess you've gotten used to that."

"And you've come in to tell me I'm too comfortable?"

Bram stopped. "Take the money. I'll go right now."

"But the Pagans . . ."

"I don't give a shit about the Pagans," he yelled. "I'll take them all on."

CHAPTER 8

DAMAGE CASE

Christ. Sweet could see that Bram was shaking, rage and hurt and grief and pain. No doubt feeling like he was going insane.

But Bram wasn't crazy—he was just so goddamned broken that he didn't care anymore. He'd let all the anger and hurt and grief pile up inside of him until he had no choice but to act on them. And he was asking Sweet for help—not with word, but with body language, and Sweet saw it as clearly as if Bram had spoken out loud. Sweet had been in this position before, with another man at another time. Different circumstances. Same needs.

So Sweet wrestled him to the ground, a fast move and then held him there so he couldn't struggle too hard and re-injure himself. Bram was strong, but seeing his scars yesterday sobered Sweet completely to what Bram had been through.

But there were plenty of ways to torture. Sweet would make sure Bram enjoyed every one of them.

"Let me up," Bram demanded.

"I would if that's what you wanted," Sweet said calmly, staring into Bram's dark eyes, noting the flush of anger and arousal that spread across his cheeks.

Sweet had lots of regular sex—sometimes more hard-core than others, but this? No, this was like the old days, with a man who'd haunted his nights for so long he'd never expected to be rid of him.

But the solid, broken man under him had the drive, the fight . . . and the need for helplessness that Sweet craved. And the feel of Bram, helpless and strong and writhing under him. Needing him—begging him for it *harderfastermorenow*. That's what motivated Sweet to push Bram right up to the edge of his limits. He didn't have the time or will to look for anything to tie Bram down. He relied on his hold and Bram's wants to get his ultimate goal.

"Take your jeans down," he growled into Bram's ear, then bit his lobe hard.

Bram shuddered and struggled to get himself free of his jeans while Sweet bit his shoulder through the cotton of his shirt.

Bram was panting but managed to get his jeans halfway down his thighs.

"Don't move," Sweet warned as he eased back in order to yank off Bram's shoes so he could get him naked. Bram let him but of course had to push things after that, grabbing Sweet by his rocker and pulling him down. Sweet didn't mind being yanked forward for a kiss, because Bram kissed like a dying man seeking water, but he also needed to remember who was in charge.

So after he let Bram kiss him, he broke away, tugged Bram's shirt over his head and kept his arms wound up in it, making it easier to roll him onto his belly while keeping his arms over his head and immobile. The soft rug under them would cushion Bram but also bite and burn, and Sweet figured that was the best of both worlds.

Bram was in pain and shaky from the meds and didn't want to give away his full fighting repertoire. But Sweet got the upper hand with no signs of relinquishing it.

"Yeah Sweet—do it," he murmured once Sweet wrestled him onto his belly more gently than Bram would've liked but still hard enough to let him know Sweet was in charge.

Bram always liked it like this, but it'd been a long time since he'd trusted anyone enough to take him this hard. Not since a few guys from his Army days took him to a leather club and introduced him to the pleasures of pain. But the ATF, and his undercover work, ensured him not being able to enjoy shit or trust anyone.

It should be the same with Sweet. If anything, he should trust Sweet less. Instead, he was letting the man hold him down, treat him like a rag doll.

Because you need it.

Sweet's hold stopped his mind from running on its hamster wheel, gave him some physical sensation besides the pain and worry that had taken up permanent residence inside of him.

This was like a drug, the perfect hit to his system, and it reached farther than any pain medication ever had.

It was far more satisfying too. A much better addiction. Safer?

Not a chance. But he was letting Sweet take him to the edge anyway.

Held down on the floor, half-naked . . . this was the release and all the pain, anger, rage and worry of the past days and months and years would let itself out on this floor, would exorcize itself on the altar of Sweet's dick and he would beg for the honor. "Fuck me, Sweet."

The growl Sweet let out was low and dangerous as he unzipped his jeans and pulled them down, freeing his dick. He bent and bit Bram's neck hard, then sucked the same spot, making the line between pain and pleasure blur. While Bram was distracted by that, Sweet had put on a condom and began to open Bram up with lubed fingers and Bram was spreading his legs wide, ready to take this man in as hard as he wanted it.

Sweet lifted his hips with a lazy strength and slid his cock in the cleft between Bram's ass, back and forth and finally—finally—he slid his thick cock until he was pushed balls-deep inside of Bram.

Bram groaned as Sweet remained still for a long moment, and Bram felt the sense of restrained violence as Sweet began to thrust against him, a rutting bull, hitting his gland.

Pleasure speared him from belly to core. A nameless emotion overwhelmed him as Sweet took him forcefully, fucking the breath out of him. Bram couldn't do anything but give in to it, let Sweet hold him down and take him for his own pleasure.

"Come back to Havoc with me," Sweet murmured against his cheek. "Don't fight it."

It was too much . . . until it wasn't. Until he nearly floated in a daze of contentment that threatened to wash all the hurt and pain away.

He struggled against it, because he couldn't allow himself to have that kind of release.

No choice left—nowhere left to run. He just let himself go, gave himself to Sweet and "Yes, Sweet . . . yes . . . *yesyesyes*please," he heard himself beg as his hips rocked back against Sweet's cock wildly, his nails digging into the rug. He couldn't get enough, an insatiable beast rising up to meet Sweet's own. Because Sweet's beast equaled his now, like he'd been starved of this for years.

And maybe he had, because this? Wasn't normal sex. Not at all. This was out-of-control, wild-as-fuck, a heartbeat-in-his-balls fucking. They'd crossed a line tonight. There was no going back.

Bram wondered if he even wanted to.

Sweet was rubbing his back, the scars, and instead of tensing up, Bram simply lay there, letting the touch run through him like tiny bolts of electricity. His skin was on fire, tight and hot, and everything ached in just the right places. He felt far away, like he was slightly floating, only coming back when Sweet said his name a couple of times.

"Bram . . . you okay?" Sweet asked again. He'd rolled off Bram and was lying next to him, and Bram was still on his belly.

"Yeah, sorry. I'm all right." He turned his head toward Sweet, still seeing stars. "Feels like my bell's been rung."

And it had. He was shaky. Unsteady. Sore . . . and yet completely satisfied in that boneless, content way a good fucking gave him.

The same electricity that ran between them that first night had never really abated but after this? There was no denying it. It was want, need, attraction, all rolled into one giant MC presidential ball.

As if to put a fine point to Bram's thoughts, Sweet leaned in and kissed him, tugging Bram's bottom lip between his teeth, like he was telling Bram, *Yes, you're right . . . now what are you going to do about it?*

He didn't expect safety from Sweet—wasn't looking for it, either. He *wanted* rough. Unsafe.

That's exactly what an MC would give him in totality. Pain to override pain was seductive. Unbelievably so.

Bram leaned into the kiss like a drowning man seeking salvation. He didn't have the strength to do anything more, even though his dick was apparently ready and able.

The fucker. "You don't play fair."

Sweet gave him a half smile. "I know."

An hour later, Bram woke with a start, his face against Sweet's shoulder, his body sore as fuck and not just in the good places.

He groaned.

"I won't take it personally that you fell asleep," Sweet told him.

"Your fault."

"You needed it. Heard you didn't sleep much last night."

"Word travels fast," Bram muttered, sitting up despite the pain, looking for his clothes. It was still light out—there were no curtains on the windows and he heard motorcycles outside. "Did we have an audience?"

"Do you care?"

Fuck it. He shook his head.

"Bram, I told them to watch out for us while we're in here. Linc's address isn't a secret."

Shit. Maybe his coming here was the stupidest idea ever. "All I wanted was time to get my shit together," he said tiredly. "Thought I had it."

"You will," Sweet assured him. "And then what? Back to the job?"

Bram shrugged. "That decision was the *getting my shit together* part." Soldiers got shot daily in the field, got patched up, and went back into the fire for more. He'd been a soldier and was applying that mentality to his current job, but for what? At what cost?

Sweet broke into his thoughts. "Is it worth it . . . what you do?"

"Stop people from doing illegal things?" Bram asked, the tinge of sarcasm clearly not lost on Sweet.

"People are always going to do illegal things." Sweet stared at him. "You're in no shape to save the world."

"Can we cut the daddy shit and just find Linc?"

"You want the daddy shit, Bram?" Sweet raised a brow and Bram's cheeks flushed. "I'll tuck that away for later."

"Bet you will," he muttered as Sweet smiled and threw Bram his jeans.

They got dressed quickly, and with Linc's mail and the cover of Sweet's men, led by Tug and Ozzie, Bram followed Sweet into his truck. Before they drove off he gave it one last shot. He reached for his wallet and pulled out the money order for the full amount of the bond and held it out to Sweet.

"You already agreed to come back to Havoc," Sweet reminded him.

"I know. I'm not reneging on that. But if you take this, then we're even."

"It's not that simple."

Bram laughed, stared up at the sky through the open sunroof. "Not that simple? It's so fucking simple."

"Even you don't believe that anymore." Sweet paused after he started the truck and repeated an earlier question. "Who hurt you, Bram?"

This time, Bram would have to answer.

It was like the game three truths and one lie. Bram was an expert at it, knew that if he put enough truth behind the story, the lie became inconsequential, nothing to worry about because it had the truth snugly wrapped around it for protection.

In this case, the lie was who he worked for. "My supervisor turned on me. Sold me out to my source I was meeting about a job. They moved the timeline up, probably so I didn't get spooked. I should've seen it coming but . . ." He shook his head, swallowed hard. "But I didn't. Thought I could handle everything."

Sweet stared straight ahead. "Being betrayed cuts the deepest."

As Sweet began to drive, Bram closed his eyes and let the irony wash over him like a cold rain.

CHAPTER 9

HEATSEEKER

"**Y**ou didn't get to see much of the place yet," Sweet commented a half an hour later as he drove onto Havoc's compound with a wave at the guards. Halfway up the first hill, Bram noted the bikes following them broke off, veering toward one of the side roads as Sweet continued along his path.

"Is this all Havoc?"

"We own the whole lot," Sweet confirmed. "Have for generations."

"It's beautiful land." And that was something he never thought he'd say about an MC compound.

"I think so too." It was obvious Sweet was proud of the place, of his club, of its members. That was also something Bram never thought he'd see in such an outright display. As they drove though the busier part of town before they got onto the compound, Sweet pointed out some Havoc-run businesses like a tattoo shop and a liquor store. On the Havoc compound itself was a diner and a few shops, including the mechanics, and it appeared that everyone here—including Sweet—seemed happy. In a rough, biker way, of course. No one was skipping through the fields and singing, and he was sure there were rough times, but the mood of the place was generally a positive one.

And there was no way a place this big would—or could—put on an act for a stranger. There was no reason to. In fact, they should be doing what they could to avoid having more strangers come into their world.

Even though he knew Havoc rarely recruited from the outside, Bram also knew through the grapevine (aka Linc) that his friend, Sean Rush, had recently been made an honorary, on the way to being official, MC member. He'd been the last guy let in within the past ten years who wasn't born into the MC.

It was also obvious, just from the short drive, how self-sufficient the place was. But that was probably the goal from the start. A way to give a military man a place where he could feel like he was still among his brothers.

Havoc's founders realized that it was impossible to come from a combat situation and be expected to land into a normal life seamlessly or unscathed. It didn't work. MCs recognized that, and thrived off it, but Havoc took it a step further. It helped the town, but it made sure its compound was self-sustaining.

Although Bram wondered why Sweet felt comfortable enough to show him Havoc's inner workings, he was also eager to see the world Linc talked about, albeit briefly.

"They accepted Rush. They were cool to me . . ."

Bram recalled treading lightly during that conversation, and worrying. *"They're not trying to recruit you, are they?"*

Linc laughed. "I'm done with joining any kind of organized group. The military cured me of that urge. But hanging out with Havoc's pretty cool."

Linc hadn't mentioned Gypsy specifically at that point. Maybe he would've, if Bram hadn't gotten beaten into an unconscious pulp and fallen off the face of the earth.

Now, as they drove farther along, the sense of calm that pervaded the land settled over both of them. "That's my cabin, behind the clubhouse."

"It's great."

"Yeah," Sweet agreed. "My sanctuary. The whole compound is that for me—for all of us."

"Linc mentioned that." So different from the Heathens, where the compound made Bram feel like he was constantly in the throes of a panic attack. It was a dark and vicious place, meant to intimidate all its members, keep them in line and make them not only suspicious of each other, but of all outsiders as well. Everything was a competition—a constant game of Russian roulette, life and death.

He had a brief flashback of one such game, when Bones killed another Heathen in front of Bram for no real reason except Bones was in a shitty mood. So in Bram's experience, all MCs were dark, lonely places. Cultlike, with egomaniacs for leaders and women beaten down by the lifestyle.

By comparison, Havoc seemed great, but Bram wasn't a member. Once patched in, it had to be dark and shitty, just like the rest of them. Speaking of, he noticed that his truck had been parked here at Sweet's, and he reminded himself to check for bugs and bombs later.

But he still got out of Sweet's truck and took a look around before going to the cabin. The main clubhouse was surrounded by a variety of structures, both traditional houses and cabins. Sweet's cabin was on the eastern side. Plenty of land and privacy and lots of windows, ensuring that he could see everyone and everything coming his way from his vantage point on the hill.

Sweet let him take it all in and then continued talking, part explanation and, Bram couldn't help but feel, part warning. "This place, this MC . . . it's more than just a club. It's my family. I know you understand family."

Bram did. What he didn't ever have a good grasp of—or trust for—was authority. "Linc and I, we have loyalty. My sister too. I've got a good friend who works the same types of jobs and I trust him with my life. But the people who were supposed to take care of me? My boss . . . my father . . ." He shook his head, wondering why the hell he was telling Sweet this shit, like the guy was his goddamned therapist.

"My dad went off the rails," Sweet offered as they walked up onto the porch of the cabin and inside. "Not hard to do with the lifestyle Havoc offers. But we're supposed to be stronger. Able to resist all the temptation that could ruin a man."

Bram glanced around the open space, noticing the framed pictures on the back wall. He saw a picture of Sweet with two men in MC jackets that resembled Sweet himself. "Was he good to you?"

It was an odd question, but Sweet seemed to understand why Bram had asked it. "He was an addict. I had my grandfather and my club. My dad didn't hit me. He was more depressed because of the loss of my mom. Hell, he loved her. Never got over her death. How can I blame him? I mean, I used to, until—" He stopped short, shook his head. "I'm older and wiser. I know nothing's black-and-white."

Bram didn't know what made him point to the picture he'd just come across, a young soldier in BDUs with his arms around Sweet and a wry smile on his face and ask, "That soldier—he show you gray?" All Sweet did was nod, but he didn't meet Bram's eyes, and then Bram didn't want to talk about the man who made Sweet try to pull away. "Linc's dad, my stepdad, was a fucking bastard. Came into my life when I was four. By the time I was ten, Linc was five and both of us caught the belt regularly. I was getting punched too. Mainly to keep Linc out of the line of fire. Kid had a mouth on him . . ."

"Still does," Sweet confirmed.

"And it doesn't mean he deserved the beatings he got," Bram said fiercely.

"I agree with you." Sweet put heavy hands on Bram's shoulders and began to massage the tension out of them. Or at least he attempted to—Bram was so tense he felt like he could easily break in two without much of a push.

"Guy was a fuck," Bram continued. "Linc's just . . . spirited."

"He's a criminal," Sweet pointed out. "But Gypsy doesn't just fall for random skips. He'd never done that in his entire career. And I know there's no love lost between you two . . . but you're on the same side."

Bram didn't believe that, not at fucking all. But he didn't say that, just kept looking around Sweet's place. It was big. Masculine. Clean. Bram counted four bedrooms on the first floor and several baths, a great room plus a large connected kitchen with a table in the middle to balance it all.

Sweet's bedroom was a loft that was almost the entire second floor, built so he could take advantage of the view. There was a giant bed on one end, and a big couch on the other, both angled to highlight the scenery. "It's gorgeous."

"Yeah, thinking the same thing." Sweet came up from behind him and kissed him on the side of his neck.

The big biker was fucking courting him. It made Bram suddenly feel shy. Nervous. Why did this matter? They'd already fucked. Why was this so much more intimate?

When was the last time you were in a guy's bedroom?

A hell of a long time ago. Bram had typically moved from one guy to the next, and happily so. He'd had no time or desire for anything more. He'd wanted sex and action and he got the latter from his job and the occasional BDSM club.

But there was something about Sweet . . . he was big and rough and handsome, and he made Bram feel vulnerable, he realized. Not physically, because Bram could take down a goddamned bull . . . but the way Sweet looked at him . . .

Dammit, you're not a blushing virgin.

He turned into Sweet and kissed him hard, trying to wrest back some control—*any* control. Sweet let him for a few moments, then motioned toward the bathroom. "Let's try out the shower. Work out the kinks."

Bram snorted but he followed, because a hot shower sounded good. Distracting. He hadn't taken a pill in a while and he didn't want to, so he hoped this was a good alternative.

He'd also been semihard since leaving Linc's. Sweet definitely kept him on edge, sexually and otherwise, and Bram wasn't sure if it was intentional or not.

Sweet led Bram into the shower, turned on the hot water and let it get steamed up while he stripped Bram and himself. Bram looked tired—half stress and true exhaustion, Sweet supposed, and he ushered the man under the water and began to soap him up.

Bram groaned as Sweet massaged his shoulders with soapy fingers, letting his head drop forward. Bram had his arm out, palm against the tile to brace himself as the water jetted out from all sides of the shower. Sweet washed both of them down, and Bram let him wash his hair, his dick, his ass, like he was docile.

Sweet knew what a crock of shit that was, but he'd take advantage of it while he could. Didn't plan on letting Bram out of bed for more than a piss and shower because he was wound way too tight.

For now, Sweet contented himself with rubbing his finger along the crack of Bram's ass. "Feels good, baby?"

Bram nodded, head still down, body becoming more pliable the longer he stayed under the hot spray.

Sweet leaned in to murmur, "I'm going to dry you off. Put you on my bed. Spread your ass and fuck it with my fingers and tongue. Want to hear the sound you make when I press deeper—open you wider. Want to see that damned blush I know will be on your cheeks."

"Fuck. Sweet . . ." Bram half turned his face to glance at Sweet and yeah, Bram wanted that.

"I warned you about the foreplay."

"Trying to kill me," Bram half groaned.

Trying to save you, Sweet thought automatically as he turned the shower off and grabbed a towel to dry them both off.

Finally, he shoved Bram's body down on the bed, lifted his hips as Bram whimpered. Sweet couldn't resist—he bent down, spread Bram and buried his face in Bram's ass.

Bram stiffened, then howled as Sweet's tongue took him, over and over. His dick thrust air, and he moaned for any kind of friction so he could come. Sweet reached around and wrapped his hand around Bram's cock, stroking it slowly as he slid his cock between Bram's ass cheeks. Sweet had Bram where he wanted him, where he needed him to be, and he didn't plan on letting him up until Bram was incoherent. The sound of bikes purring in the background was the perfect backdrop . . . until Bram went still underneath him, tension filling his body and Sweet froze on top of him, waiting.

The sudden sound of Harleys roaring through Sweet's opened windows ripped Bram out of his pleasure haze. Loud. A pack of them. Bearing down . . .

They're here to kill you.

But they weren't. He was with Havoc, not Heathens, and Sweet was about to fuck him, Bram reasoned.

Suddenly, being trapped under Sweet's body, in Sweet's house, on Sweet's MC compound was just too fucking much. Every other time, they'd been on a more neutral ground. Even at Gypsy's, Bram was still in town.

Now, he was on MC land. Virtually trapped. Prisoner. And even though he'd allowed himself to be pulled deeper and deeper into Havoc, he still had to prove he had a choice in this.

He shifted and stilled . . . and, instinctively, so did Sweet.

How much of your ass does Sweet really expect? How little would he deal with? Bram needed those answers and he grabbed the headboard for leverage as he prepared for a different kind of fight.

Sweet heard Bram's whimper above the growl of the bikes, and something about the tone made Sweet stop and wait. They'd been together enough times for Sweet to know that wasn't a sound of pleasure. So he let Bram shift, even pull away, although he didn't loosen his own hold all that much.

It was like Bram needed to know that he could get away. Needed to prove it.

Well hell, Sweet needed to prove he'd never fuck anyone against their will. And when Bram turned to face him, he stared back at Bram with all the patience he could muster.

Bram seemed to waver between fighting Sweet and letting himself be fucked . . . and Sweet waited for him to make that decision. Finally, Sweet murmured, "I'll move away."

But Bram shook his head and struck hard with panther-like movement, flipping and dropping on Sweet. Which was damned hard to do. Sweet wasn't going to let Bram hurt him, but he hadn't realized how damned strong the man actually was.

Bram was breathing hard, sitting on Sweet's chest, and for a moment, his eyes were unfocused. Haunted, like he was waking up from a nightmare.

Sweet, in turn, murmured, "Come on, Bram. You want to take me? Go ahead, baby. Take what you need."

"Is that what you do—take what you need?" Bram asked.

"Sometimes. When you're willing," Sweet conceded.

"You're not in fucking charge of me."

Sweet gave him a dark smile. "Think again, babe. I'm pretty much calling all the shots, pulling all your goddamned strings while you're a guest of Havoc's. And when my dick's inside of you, I'm not hearing a whole lot of complaints. But I'm not into forcing anyone to fuck . . . unless they like pretending they need to be forced."

That seemed to ease something in Bram, cemented the fact that he needed the push-pull during sex the way he needed air. Sweet had seen it before, understood it—and Bram—maybe better than Bram himself did. Because then Bram leaned in, put his forehead on Sweet's and then angled his head so he could kiss Sweet. Holding him in place like he did that first night when he'd pushed Sweet against the wall. Kissing the shit out of him.

When he broke the kiss, he murmured, "You can be in charge—in here. Right now."

After Bram spoke, Sweet wasted no time in flipping him onto his back and mounting him. His legs straddled Bram's hips, Bram's legs spread around his thighs as Sweet's hand stroked his ass.

Bram closed his eyes, felt the bed shift, heard the snap of the lube cap. He took a deep, stuttered breath, his dick hard as hell. "Come on, Sweet. Hurry."

He braced himself, hands clutching the sheets by his sides as Sweet stretched him with lube-slicked fingers.

"Put your hands on the headboard. Grab the bars," Sweet ordered and Bram resisted . . . for a moment. In return, Sweet bent down and bit his nipples, causing Bram to surge up, gritting his teeth in pain . . . and pleasure.

"Fuck," Bram bit out in response, renewing his grip on the sheets.

Sweet stared at him. "Hands. Up."

"Or what?"

"I'll flip you. Tie you. Spank you until you can't sit comfortably for days," Sweet warned, then leaned in to whisper, "Or maybe that's exactly what you want."

Bram groaned, despite himself. His hands went up to grasp the bars of the headboard and Sweet entered him quickly. The pinch, the pressure, the pain was all so fucking good and necessary, and Bram fought the urge to yell or howl as Sweet grabbed his hips and began to pump hard and fast.

He'd never trusted anyone in charge of him because he'd never had a reason to. He knew trusting Sweet beyond fucking was a death wish, but that just made this fucking so much better. He wrapped his legs around Sweet, heels digging into Sweet's broad back, and let himself go up in flames.

Bram opened his eyes slowly. Sweet was still on his knees, in no hurry to move, looking him up and down unabashedly. Bram's come was sticky on his belly, and he knew he looked well-fucked, could see it reflected in Sweet's eyes.

Finally, Sweet moved off him, and Bram watched him get rid of the condom before lying down next to Bram on the bed. "Another shower, then we get moving."

"Maybe I want to stay dirty," Bram told him.

Sweet snorted. "Don't worry—you will."

Bram thought about keeping his next thoughts to himself, then realized he couldn't. "Do you do this a lot?"

"What?"

"Take non-MC strangers into your home."

"No. But because of Sean, Linc's practically family."

"Because family borrows money and never pays it back?" Bram shot out without thinking, and thankfully, Sweet laughed.

"Pretty much sums it up, doesn't it?" He sighed. "The last man here with me was the solider you saw in the picture—his name was James. Jimmy-Boy."

Was. Shit. "Combat?"

Sweet nodded slowly. "Jimmy-Boy was a good man, but he was fucked in his own way. Like you, he loved danger. And me. He just chose one over the other exclusively."

"I'm sorry, Sweet."

"So am I."

"So there's been no one since Jimmy?"

"A lot of someones, but not like that," Sweet admitted. "You?"

"Nah. Between the military and the job, not a lot of downtime. One-night stands worked best."

Bram used *worked*—past tense. And what if he did? It's not like there was a future here . . .

Not even if Bram thought he wanted one. "I need to find . . ."

"Linc. I know." Sweet paused. "You use that like a shield."

Bram couldn't deny the truth in that. Because even though finding Linc was tantamount, Sweet knew it. Bram repeating it seven million times?

Shield. "Been a rough month."

"Yep. I know that too," Sweet said quietly. "Just consider what I'm saying."

All Bram could do was nod.

CHAPTER 10

THE PLEASURE IS TO PLAY

Sweet walked over to the diner Fay ran on Havoc's property. Bram had turned over and waved him away when Sweet offered him food, and Sweet took the opportunity, because he had a lot of shit to do today, including checking up on the gas station Linc visited before he disappeared. He texted Ozzie and Tug to meet him in the clubhouse in ten and figured he'd find Gypsy at Fay's to catch him up as well.

As always, the pride he felt in Havoc tightened his chest a little as he walked the short distance through the busiest parts of the compound. At times growing up he'd simultaneously loved and hated this place, but he knew now that there wasn't anyplace else that could possibly be better for him than here.

A lot of men who joined the MC didn't have an easy time of it growing up, and although Sweet was considered a legacy, his time coming up was as difficult as any of his men's. He'd figured out he was gay at an early age, and although his grandfather had been as well, that didn't make things any less confusing. Throw in a shitty father and a good but tough grandfather who had a compound to run, and Sweet had ended up a tough but extremely angry kid. His grandfather sired kids but didn't marry. Relationships were kept secret, more because he'd wanted to protect those close to him versus keeping his relationships with men under wraps.

Back then, Sweet hadn't been sure he'd wanted this lifestyle, despite—or maybe because of—the fact that he didn't know anything else.

When he'd left for the Marines, he'd learned quickly. At that point, he realized he did have other choices, could've stayed in the military or gotten out and gotten on with life somewhere else.

But growing up Havoc was part of his blood, and walking away? He realized that there were too many cons and far too few pros. So when he returned to Havoc, it was because he wanted to, not because he had to. Because he knew the club was where he belonged. Where he needed to be. His brothers were here. Others from the Marines followed him in. Havoc was robust. They had rogue members and an offshoot that Sean Rush and Ryker, his XO, were currently dealing with, but Sweet didn't want other charters. Havoc was special—the land she'd been built on was, and you couldn't re-create that magic. He'd rather draw from it than attempt to dilute it.

So for years, he put Havoc before himself. He'd reasoned that's what the club needed—and it had been. But when Jimmy-Boy came into his life, things changed. He tried to balance things, but Jimmy needed him and so did Havoc, since Heathens had gone into overdrive with their drug trade during that time, especially the meth. And Jimmy needed far more attention than Sweet could give him and the entire relationship tore him apart. Bad.

After Jimmy, Sweet swore off relationships and stuck to sex only, and most of the men he slept with respected that. Most of them didn't want anything more either.

Even so, Havoc was a lot to manage. Men did stupid things—for women, power, and money—and his MC, and Sweet himself, wasn't immune to those charms. He worked hard to keep it pure, to help it sustain itself and its members.

And he himself walked a fine line daily, and right now he was balancing the hell out of the tightrope because of the man currently asleep in his bed.

"I like the new guy," Fay declared.

"I'll have my usual," was Sweet's first answer. "And you haven't met him yet. And I think you're getting soft in your old age, woman."

"I like the way you smile since he came into the picture, asshole." She punctuated her words by throwing an empty can at him. He shifted and caught it before it made contact with his head. Then she pointed at him. "Don't mess this up."

"There's nothing to mess up. He's here until we find Linc."

She stared at him as he lied to her face, but she didn't call him out on it. But the look she gave him? Enough to tell him she knew everything. She poured him a mugful of coffee and pushed it his way. "Please do it soon," she said, with a pointed glance toward the corner table where Gypsy was currently glowering.

Sweet nodded, grabbed the coffee, and headed over to his friend's table. Gypsy glanced up for a second from his phone, long enough for Sweet to see the black eyes and the bandage across his broken nose. "Glad one of us is happy. But I don't need your good fucking cheer this morning."

Sweet ignored that and slid into the seat across from him. "Did Misha check that out?"

"It's fine. Not the first hits I've taken."

"You provoked him," Sweet told him evenly.

"And you didn't?" Gypsy asked without looking up at him. "Or are you going to try to convince me we're playing good cop–bad cop?"

"I'm not playing anything. He's fucked up."

"Tell me about it," Gypsy muttered, throwing his phone onto the table and lowering his voice. "What the fuck, Sweet?"

"What the fuck's your problem—besides getting your ass kicked for saying shit about Bram's brother? You had to know that wouldn't go over well."

"Stop babying him, dammit," Gypsy spat out. "You're fucking him for information—at least that's what you're supposed to be doing."

The anger balled up inside of him. "Shut it down, man. You don't run me."

"I know. I think he's running you though. He's a dangerous fucker."

"So am I."

"Great. Right now, I'm not a fan of either one of you, so I hope you know what you're doing."

Sweet sighed. "He's fucked up as hell—I know that. But so was I at one point. So were you."

Gypsy's eyes hardened. "Don't you dare compare me to him, Sweet. Don't you fucking dare."

"I just did." Sweet pushed away from the table and walked out without waiting for his breakfast. Gypsy was one of the few he allowed to question at will, because he never wanted to become a goddamned island of a leader, but he'd done nothing to compromise Havoc.

Nothing you know of.

Bram sat on Sweet's porch, watching the sun come up, thinking about how different Havoc appeared to be. Granted, most of the men here could've been ax murderers and they'd still be a nicer group than what he'd witnessed over the past years.

That shit was enough to send him into a tailspin, his beating notwithstanding. All along, he'd been forced to watch Bones order his men to torture other MC members, and some innocents from town, and incite fear wherever the Heathens went. The night he'd finally pulled out (earlier than anticipated but longer than most would've lasted) was right before he was supposed to kill someone in order to get his patch. The big payout for that would've been an introduction to the inner circle and possibly a face-to-face with the main kingpin of the heroin trade that the Heathens were trying to break into.

The worst part was that he'd been expected to patch in. The ATF—Parisi specifically—wanted him to. For the greater good. Kill one, save many. But Bram had justified too many damned things in his life, and that one wouldn't balance anything out. He'd spent too much time sitting on his hands, hating himself and everyone around him, including the ATF, for having to do so. Would the same happen here?

You won't be here that long, he reminded himself. Not at the rate Parisi was moving to track him down. Bram actually had begun the process of coming to terms with dying, maybe before he found Linc. The scariest part?

He wasn't all that goddamned scared. Dying might be the easiest thing he'd ever done.

So while he was at Havoc, he needed to make the best of it, make it work for him for Linc's sake.

Linc. Fuck. He couldn't shake the suspicion that Heathens had something to do with Linc's disappearance, but wouldn't Havoc know that by now? Or Parisi? Heathens wanted to torture Bram—the best way to do it was to let him know that they had his brother.

But it was radio silence on all fronts. Short of busting into Heathens, aka certain death, he'd have to continue letting Havoc do his dirty work for him.

And speaking of dirty, yeah, it felt good to be able to give up control to Sweet, to stop looking over his shoulder for even those few moments he allowed himself to do so.

After two years of being surrounded by scum, of having to watch his back, he was actually letting himself think he could trust Sweet.

Which was ridiculous.

It was risk-taking behavior, but hell, he wasn't related to Linc for nothing. He'd agreed to go undercover, so of course he had that gene in common with his brother, as hard as he pretended he didn't.

The military might've forced him into the straight and narrow path, until Special Forces. And then it was a different set of rules, although all of it required control. Precision. Deadly calm.

He was decorated. He'd taken out a lot of bad men and saved a lot of good ones. But he'd also seen more than his fair share of horrors and, at thirty-two, felt old as fuck.

The next steps, whatever they might be, appeared currently unattainable. Instead, he'd let himself relax in Sweet's cabin.

In Sweet's bed.

He hadn't wanted to meet—or possibly *like*—any of these people. Didn't need to be taken in and adopted like a stray fucking puppy. Because it wasn't real. He wasn't real.

It's the realest role you've played in years, he reminded himself. He was a man searching for his brother and seeking help from the last people who'd seen him. He *knew* that trusting Sweet—or any MC member—was Stockholm-level stupidity. They were together because Bram needed the grounding that sex with Sweet gave him, and Sweet was looking for intel—on both Linc and Bram.

Thing was, they were also both seeking a way into each other. It was working . . . but it was going to backfire and really fucking soon. Because they'd both realized it was much more than either man wanted, and they'd learned that from the first night they'd fucked outside Bertha's.

Sweet didn't bother waiting for Gypsy at the clubhouse. Ozzie and Tug met him there and he briefed them on the bank account information and sent them to the gas station Linc's bank statement showed, told them to keep it on the QT. Fay had dropped off his breakfast, and so he sat at the head of the long clubhouse table and began to eat.

Gypsy walked in about ten minutes later. Sweet hoped his friend had cooled down, but one look told him that was wishful thinking.

Sweet motioned for the probie named Callum, who was currently cleaning up behind the bar, to leave them alone, which he did with a nod. Gypsy sat next to him and said, "Is Bram alone in your house?"

"Yes."

Gypsy shook his head. "Playing it cool—I get it. But come the fuck on—this guy's a problem. For you and for Havoc."

"Nothing to do with your broken nose, right?" he asked and Gypsy glared at him, then softened.

"I don't want you hurt, Sweet."

"Yeah well, it happens." He knew Gypsy wasn't only thinking about Linc, but about Jimmy-Boy as well. Havoc had accepted Jimmy-Boy in with open arms because Sweet loved him. Sweet had learned that loving something didn't always mean it was good for you, but he'd let go of his guilt a while ago. "But I hear you. I know exactly what Bram is."

Bram was most dangerous because he could pass for an easygoing guy. He was tall but not especially broad, but the way the man moved at times . . . it was obvious he was a trained machine. Sleek, silent. Sweet could see him moving in for the kill.

But Bram was also broken, and it had little to do with the scars Sweet had seen on him that first night. Something else had taken place and robbed the man of some of his soul. Sweet had seen that too often, and he'd also lived it.

Why Bram tugged at him when no one had for so damned long was anyone's guess. He decided to change the subject. "We found Linc's bank statement," he started and Gypsy watched him cautiously. "There was a charge at a gas station an hour away—over the border. Nothing else after that. No sign of any credit card statements beyond the one we know was his."

Gypsy nodded slowly. "So you agreed to help him."

"Based on what we found? I told him that I'd check things out."

Gypsy shifted, giving him a hard look. "You really think something happened to him?"

"It's a hell of a setup if it did."

"People will do a lot of shit for money."

"Bram's got the bond money. He's got a money order all ready." Sweet glanced at his phone. "Ozzie's on his way back from the gas station—says he's got news. I'm guessing it's getting to be time to make some serious calls."

"Rumors about Linc will get out to Heathens soon enough," Gypsy warned. "Is that what you're looking for?"

"Yes," Sweet said decisively.

"Why would they hold a hostage and not ask for anything?" Gypsy wondered.

"I don't know," Sweet answered honestly. "You sure you're ready to find out?"

"Are you?"

Sweet didn't bother to answer, continued eating as they put aside their Bram differences for the moment. Gypsy filled him in on updates, news on other MCs that Bram might've missed, and a report on Ryker and Rush's current operation that'd kept them away from Havoc for the past several months.

They needed Ryker back here—the big man brought a real sense of balance to Havoc that was sorely needed at the moment.

After an hour of going over books and such, Gypsy nodded as Ozzie opened the clubhouse door. "Hey boss—think you're going to want to see this."

Both Sweet and Gypsy rose from the table and went to join Ozzie outside. Once there, Sweet saw Bram was walking along the path toward the clubhouse—Sweet had told him to do so after he showered, but he noted that Bram slowed down a bit when he saw them, like he knew this wasn't a conversation he needed to be a part of.

"Inside," Sweet told him, but not before realizing that Ozzie and Tug had unloaded Linc's bike from their truck. They left it parked out front, and Sweet stood by the window and said, "Talk."

"Guy saw the van—saw guys like me take another guy off a bike and figured it was MC shit," Ozzie confirmed. "Then he profited by taking Linc's bike and making it his."

"And now?"

"He's planning on relocating," Ozzie said. "He got the make and model of the van, no plates and no evidence of what MC took Linc."

"So he was going to sit on it, thinking it was club business," Sweet mused. "Was he in on it?"

Tug shook his head. "Don't think so. Just benefitted from it."

Sweet watched as Bram approached the bike hesitantly at first before touching it almost reverently.

Gypsy saw it too, gave a low whistle. "Guy is fucked up."

Sweet couldn't disagree, anymore than he could cut Bram loose. "Time to make some calls."

"Anyone specific?" Tug asked.

"Virgil." Because if Virgil knew, then Sweet could be assured it was true.

Sweet approached Bram, who was still holding on to the bike as if it were a lifeline, and told him what his men learned. It wasn't all that hard convincing Bram to stay behind, especially when he gave Bram permission to ride around Havoc grounds. And a mere half an hour later, Sweet, Tug, and Ozzie were back out on the road, headed to meet Virgil in one of their safe houses. Heavily guarded, with a Laundromat as a front, very few outside Havoc's inner circle knew about the meeting room in the back.

Virgil was one of the few. He was from the Sons of Bastards MC, a rogue member who could always be counted on to keep the SOBs, Havoc, and Hangmen from getting caught up in Heathen and Pagan shit. Former Special Forces, the guy was like a goddamned shadow, which was the only reason he was still alive.

Plus he was a slick goddamned bastard. If he didn't trust you, he'd kill you without a second glance.

The alley behind the Laundromat led to a private, locked lot that was always guarded. Sweet and the others were ushered in with their bikes, and Virgil was let in moments later, on foot.

"We going in?" Tug asked.

"No. Better out here." Sweet never liked being cornered. He trusted Virgil but this wasn't his first rodeo. His safety—and that of his men—came first. The Laundromat held civilians. With the tension between Havoc and Pagans, it was best if Sweet wasn't seen or heard anywhere near here.

Virgil wore dark glasses that he propped on his green bandanna–wrapped head. His eyes were ice-blue, days' worth of scruff stubbled his chin and cheeks, and he was head-to-toe road leather. He held out his hand to Sweet, then Ozzie and Tug respectively.

The latter two remained for the conversation, but only to listen. "Thanks for coming so quickly, Virgil."

"You caught me right before I left town. Lucky you." He gave a half smile full of irony and jumped right in. "I've got it on excellent knowledge that Heathens tried to kill a probie who turned traitor and tried to escape the night of his patch initiation. They want him back alive and they're willing to pay."

Sweet processed the information without changing his expression, a trick he'd perfected early on when he'd learned that emotion didn't equal weakness, but showing it was always interpreted as so. "And?"

"Same good authority pinpointed his locale. To Shades." Virgil shrugged and pulled his glasses down to stare at Sweet. "Know anything about that?"

"Not a thing. But I'll keep my eyes peeled." Both men knew damned well that Havoc wouldn't do shit for the Heathens, no matter how much they were paying. "But the guy I'm looking for wasn't a Heathen probie. It was Linc."

"Yeah. Met him a coupla times. Good guy." Virgil shrugged. "Heard he skipped bail. Heard something about fucking with credit cards too."

Sweet's gut tightened. He and Gypsy had kept that information on the down-low—at least on Havoc's end. Would Linc have been stupid enough to fuck with other MCs? "I'll keep an ear to the ground on that, but for now, any sign of Linc, you'll call, yeah?"

"You know I will." Virgil held out his hand and Sweet shook it. "Always a goddamned pleasure, Sweet."

Tug and Ozzie didn't say a word. Not until Virgil left the premises and Sweet said, "Speak freely."

"It's pretty damned obvious the Heathen probie is Bram," Tug said bluntly.

"But he fought for us," Ozzie pointed out. "Maybe he's looking for refuge."

"And putting us in danger," Tug shot back.

They were both right. He thought about how Bram's supervisor was the one to sell him out, and wondered how the hell that tied into Bram's possible Heathen status. "Bram's Linc's brother," Sweet said carefully. "For Gypsy's sake, we need to hold Bram safe until we find Linc."

"No matter the danger to Havoc?" Tug asked seriously.

"We've faced greater," Sweet reminded him. "Let's go. Business as usual in front of Bram and the others. It's Garth's birthday—we party as planned tonight—with extra security. I'm sure other members are hearing the rumors about the Heathen probie with the bounty on his head, so the more they see me with Bram, the less they'll focus their suspicions on him. No one's turning him in without coming to me first."

Tug nodded in acknowledgment, because they all knew that if Bram was a Heathen, they'd suss it out sooner than later. But if they played their cards right, it wouldn't be until they found Linc . . . and their missing money.

CHAPTER 11

DOUBLE UP OR QUIT

Before Sweet left, Bram had asked if he could take a ride around the compound on Linc's bike. Sweet had given him two roads he could take, both of them pretty well deserted and no doubt serving this purpose, as Bram noted a few young men learning to ride their first bikes along the way. Most who encountered him just stared at him like the fucking outsider he was.

But just being on the bike—Linc's bike—stopped his panic. He hadn't been sure if riding would make it worse, but now that he was a step closer to finding his brother, this was his way of getting in touch with the universe about Linc.

Because that's the kind of shit Linc would say, how he would think about things. But when Bram's phone started to ring, he pulled over immediately.

The hairs on his arms stood on end as he yanked the phone from his pocket, because there was too much information flying around, fast and furious . . . and so far, none of it good.

He couldn't see Dozer's call being the exception.

"How's it going?" Dozer started off.

"All cool," he answered, the code they used to let the other know they were in the clear.

"Heathens know you're in Shades. From there, it's not going to be hard to put two and two together," Dozer informed him. "The MC's putting out major feelers for you—and they've put a major bounty on your head. They want you alive."

"How the fuck?"

"Someone ran a credit check on you and Linc in the past twenty-four hours—the IP address is from a business in Shades. Guy on the deed is named Jaxon George."

"I don't know that name."

"Bail bonds shop," Dozer said quietly.

"Gypsy. That motherfucker." Bram ran a hand through his hair.

"Parisi caught the search easily and turned the Heathens onto you. But I did a little more digging and found something else. I ran Gypsy's credit—there were credit cards taken out in his name about a month ago . . . maybe a week before Linc disappeared."

"Does he know?"

"He was contacted. Whoever did it? A sloppy-as-fuck job—like they wanted to get caught."

"That's not Linc's MO." He'd known Gypsy was suspicious and not without good reason. If Bram went to him about any of it now, he'd give away his hand . . . and that was about to be revealed anyway. "Sweet confirmed that Linc was taken. Kidnapped. Shoved into a van. They got his bike back from a witness who saw it all, but that's it."

"Heathens?"

"They didn't commit to anything. But fuck—I've got to get out of here."

"Agreed. But how?"

"I'll figure it out," Bram assured him.

"Get the fuck out of there tonight. I'll get coordinates to a safe house. You're going to have to lay low for a while."

"How can I do that, with Linc missing?" Bram demanded.

"You've got to be alive to find him."

Sweet got back to Havoc in time to see Bram taking another ride on Linc's bike, racing up the road like a fucking pro.

"He rides well," Tug noted after a long moment of silence among the three men in the car. "Like, better-than-a-bike-enthusiast well."

Ozzie shrugged. "Doesn't mean anything."

"Or it could mean everything," Sweet said darkly.

Sweet wished Ryker and Rush were here—if nothing else, Rush could verify things about Linc's brother. But they were incommunicado and for very good, lifesaving reasons. Sweet wouldn't risk that on something he could take care of by himself.

Were his instincts about Bram that off? *Was* Bram playing him? It was more than time to find out.

"Good ride?" Sweet asked as Bram pulled Linc's bike in front of Sweet's place.

Bram felt Sweet's energy strumming through him—and his gut told him something was off. It wasn't the time to push for intel—not too hard, anyway. So he got off the rebuilt Harley and answered carefully, "Very. Linc and I grew up riding my dad's bikes. It's been a while, but I guess you never forget. Speaking of . . .?"

"I put the word out about Linc but my source didn't hear anything," Sweet told him, and Bram pretended to accept what he suspected was a partial lie. Still, he didn't think that Sweet would have information about where Linc was and not tell Bram, so this was something more, and likely what he and Doz had discussed.

"Okay. I'm going to ride for a while longer—"

Sweet started walking into the house and motioned for him to follow. "Come on and shower up. We're celebrating Garth's birthday in a few."

"I'm not in the party mood," Bram told him, but he walked into the house behind Sweet, followed him up the stairs.

"Doesn't matter. Club rules," Sweet countered.

"Club rules," Bram echoed hollowly. "Right. But I'm not a part of your club."

Sweet's hand was on his chest, stopping him. "You're with me. I am the club. A problem with the club means a problem with me."

"I guess we've got a problem then," Bram said gruffly.

"You can't sit in here—you'll go crazy."

Didn't Sweet know he was already more than halfway there? "I can go looking for him."

"Right. Like that's going to get you anywhere." Sweet shook his head. "Like I said, we've got feelers out. It's better to go through the MC channels—safer, for us and for Linc."

Bram knew that he couldn't do it alone, not without a major disguise and any kind of lead. He really wanted to check out the gas station guy's story himself.

He also knew that tonight's party represented an opportunity for him to escape, and it might be his only chance.

He'd get the hell out of here, mail Havoc the money order on his way out of town, and then spend the next weeks avoiding the Heathens and looking for Linc.

And then . . .

He shook his head. *Don't think that far in advance.*

Sweet broke into his thoughts. "You've got that look in your eyes again."

"What look?"

"Like you're about to hyperventilate."

He glanced up at Sweet and saw the genuine concern there. "I'll be fine."

"I don't want you to be fine. I want so much more for you than that."

"Why?"

Sweet cupped the back of his neck. "I'm trying to figure that out myself, but I've learned that when the feeling hits, questioning it doesn't help."

"What does?"

Sweet smiled. "Letting me make you feel better than fine."

"It's not that easy."

"Why not?"

"You make me feel," was the best answer Bram could give. Because the feeling was way beyond anger, pain, fear, or rage. Finally, he could let someone tunnel through that to find raw, unadulterated pleasure, and that someone was Sweet.

The same Sweet who put two fingers under his chin and forced him to lock with Sweet's gaze. "That's a good thing, babe. But I get a feeling you don't think so."

Sweet was right. As much as Bram liked it, liked being controlled when he was coming, the fact that he'd given Sweet that much power over him . . .

That made him far too vulnerable. Reminded him of exactly how vulnerable he truly was. "I'm doing the best I can."

Sweet seemed to understand that. But really, with the number of secrets and lies between them, how far could this really go? It was as if the wall between them kept rising and at one point, it would become insurmountable.

Or else, he could bash through it, but he was damned tired of beating his head against proverbial walls.

Finally, he hung his head, worn out from his internal battle. His body was heavy with exhaustion, his muscles ached, his brain muddled like he could sleep forever.

"Stay with me," Sweet urged. "Don't make any decisions tonight."

Even though Bram already had, he looked at Sweet and hated feeling like he'd be willing to let his resistance melt. He wanted to let Sweet win.

But that would mean that Bram had lost.

Even so, all he did was step toward Sweet and let Sweet's mouth come down on his, a punishing kiss that took Bram's breath away, that made him alternately more nervous and horny as fuck.

Anticipation of what was to come both before and after what happened in this bedroom.

The danger balance here was a huge turn-on. Sweet might know everything. Bram needed to run. But right now, there was nothing he could do but follow what Sweet—and his own body—ordered him to do.

"Get on your hands and knees," Sweet murmured, then backed up to allow him to do so.

"No," Bram said.

Sweet didn't move. "I won't ask again. If you want it . . ."

Fuck, he did, wanted, needed to be forced into it. Sweet knew that but wouldn't do it. Ironic. Sweet would kill him for hurting Havoc but wouldn't beat him without consent.

A hoarse laugh escaped his lips, and on unsteady legs, he sank to the floor . . . on all fours.

Sweet walked around him, obviously pleased.

"Hurry the fuck up," Bram ordered.

Sweet's hand stroked his lower back, and fear and anger and the fiercest need piled up inside of Bram. A balloon that needed to burst.

Sweet could easily hold him down—and nothing was stopping him from killing Bram right now.

Bram shook, a mix of pain and fear, and Sweet noticed immediately. "You're in pain."

"Lots of it."

"Do you need your pills? Or can I try to take your mind off of it?" Sweet watched him and Bram gave the barest of nods, consenting.

Sweet's first smack was hard, stinging Bram's bare ass and then stopping. Fuck—not enough.

And Sweet knew that, used his open-handed palm to hit him, hard and fast, varying where the smacks came down and managing to put Bram into the exact place he needed to be—calm, focused on the right here and now.

Why was the man who could turn out to be the biggest threat to his existence the one who could make him the calmest?

He hung his head down, arms burning, a thin film of sweat covering his skin. Sweet leaned in, murmured, "You know how strong a man you have to be to submit," then licked along the side of his neck and Bram shivered.

It wasn't really a question, and Bram didn't feel all that strong, but it felt good to know Sweet thought that, and thought Bram a worthy adversary.

He'd have to be that and more in the next few hours. But now? All he had to do was be here. Unable to trust, wanting to belong, knowing how to fake it, to fit in . . . but that wasn't the same thing as truly finding his place somewhere. He'd spent so much of his life and career living as someone else that the only way he really knew how to live was to live in the moment.

Nothing more in the moment than this. "That all you got, Sweet?"

Sweet laughed, and then trapped him, held Bram's head down to the ground a tight wrestling-like hold that made Bram safe and vulnerable at once. Sweet's hand went half over Bram's mouth, forcing him to suck Sweet's fingertips as Sweet pounded into him flat to the mattress, invaded, impaled, and unwilling to fight.

There was no denying his body's reaction. He was drowning and flying at the same time.

Bram wanted to ask if they could stay here all night, like this, miss the party and keep fucking.

But that was putting off the inevitable. This might be Sweet's way of saying goodbye.

Or maybe you're losing your edge.

Sweet's hips snapped, driving him more deeply into Bram, and his body tensed, strung tight like a bow that Sweet was holding. Stroking. Testing. Sweet, embracing him, detaining him, fucking him with a vengeance that spread heat through Bram's entire body. He'd never felt so goddamned taken, so owned, claimed, so fucking full of Sweet's cock, of Sweet's everything.

"Take it, Bram. Take it all," Sweet groaned.

"Yes," Bram managed, his face pressed into the carpet, his ass up, unable to do anything but accept Sweet's hard thrusts.

When he came, his entire body jerked from the force of both his and Sweet's climaxes.

Bram got dressed, his body still buzzing from the sex, his mind following suit, but in a much more distracted way. Because his mind was looking for a way out, knew there wasn't a choice . . . but his body? Wanted to stay and let Sweet fuck him any way he'd like.

He needed to go. Find a way to not go to the party. Or hope that afterwards, everyone was so mellow and loose that they'd be off guard. Even slightly. If they weren't . . .

"You ready?" Sweet asked, coming out onto the porch to join him, pulling on his leather vest, wet hair tied back messily.

Ready? Definitely not. Even if escape wasn't on the table, recalling how Gypsy glared at him after talking to Sweet made his gut clench. He didn't give a shit that Gypsy was mad at him, but he didn't want to decimate Sweet's friendships either.

Which was what would happen when he escaped. Sweet would be to blame.

"Why are you fighting with Gypsy?" Bram asked him to stop his mind running.

"Just a difference of opinion. He'll get over it."

"Will you?" Bram asked.

"What do you care? You don't even want to be here, so don't get involved in shit that doesn't concern you."

"Right." Bram stared straight ahead. "I think it's better I stay at Linc's."

"It's—"

"I don't care. Fuck, I told you I'd give Gypsy the bond." Bram swore a muffled curse under his breath. "I don't belong here."

"You're here with me."

"You keep saying that. Trying to bend me to your will, to show everyone I behave for the president."

"That's not it."

"That's exactly it." Bram brought his fists hands down on the porch railing, hard enough to make them ache. The pain was welcomed. Maybe the only thing that was at the moment. "Doesn't matter if I don't like it here."

"Do you?"

"I don't belong here."

"Bram—"

"I'm not part of this community. Not looking to patch in. And I'm not fighting anyone for acceptance." Been there, done that . . . had the PSTD flashbacks to prove it. They were becoming more intense, and the fact that he was being lulled into believing that this place was different? Granted, no meth, but an MC all the same. Rules, regs, and a president everyone listened to.

Same shit, different day.

Sweet put a hand on his shoulder. "Let's go."

Bram wanted to ignore the implicit command behind the overt one, but his body refused to. He blamed the danger. His need.

He blamed Sweet. Because it should be so much easier to save himself.

Because Sweet had to know something, or at least suspect it. And Bram didn't have it in him to hide much longer. He was having a problem keeping his undercover persona up and running.

CHAPTER 12

I'M GONNA CHANGE MY EVIL WAYS

Something was off. Sweet looked around the party as though he could suss out the issue with a glance, but the rustling, restless breeze that fluttered around him remind him that shit like this wasn't always in his power.

On the outside, everyone was having fun. Things were calm—as much as any Havoc party could be considered calm, and most men and women weren't quite drunk just yet. Still, everyone seemed happy.

But, as it had so many times before, for Sweet there appeared to be an overlay that gave the entire area a grayish cast, like the land was attempting to warn him.

"What's up?" Tug asked quietly. He'd been standing with Sweet for most of the night. Ozzie was walking the crowds, listening for murmurs of anything that seemed off, and Gypsy was sitting on the closest porch by himself, brooding.

Sweet glanced at Tug. "Not sure. Perimeters okay?"

"Just swept."

"Do it again. Better yet, post men for the night."

Tug didn't argue—never would when security was a factor—and left.

He glanced over at Bram, who was somehow drunk and uptight all at once. Maybe he sensed that something was up as well, or maybe it was a guilty conscience. Sweet figured he'd find out soon enough.

Ozzie was the first to report trouble. "Spoke with Tug. Pagans are here. They say that they're looking for the Heathen probie with the bounty on his head. They want to bring him in, dead or alive. They say we're harboring a club fugitive and club rules dictate we send him back." Ozzie didn't look happy about either prospect, but he kept it professional. "They're being held at the bottom. They say they don't want trouble—if we hand him over, they won't tell the Heathens that we were the ones harboring their man."

Sweet barked a harsh laugh. "Tell them I'll come down there and piss on them if they don't get the fuck out of here."

Ozzie frowned, glanced at Bram. "But Sweet—"

"He rejected the Heathens, right?" Sweet reasoned.

"Yeah," Ozzie admitted. "This could be a Trojan horse situation though."

It could be. But Sweet refused to be bullied into anything. "Tell the motherfuckers to go on home alone."

"What if they come back with proof?" Ozzie asked. "Or with the Heathens themselves."

Sweet glanced over at Bram, who seemed blissfully unaware of the ripples running through the MC's membership. "By then, we'll know the truth."

Ozzie nodded slowly. "You up for this?"

"Yes," Sweet said firmly. "First, we save his life and then figure out of it was worth saving. Because everyone makes mistakes."

Bram had been trained to read lips, and although he was damned good at it, he found himself fading in and out as he kept his eyes on Sweet and Ozzie while they put their heads together. He caught *Pagans* and *Heathens* and his own name. And finally . . . *Everyone makes mistakes.*

Those words hit him like a kick to the sternum. He bent forward, his breath coming in hard, painfully panicked gasps. He was trapped. He'd never escape this job, and the enormity of that washed over him like a tidal wave.

He remained there alone and continued to drown mercilessly.

At some point, there were voices surrounding him. Inside, he felt oddly calm and peaceful, but his body was fighting something he didn't quite understand.

"Bram, what the fuck did you do to yourself? What did you take?" Sweet was asking harshly.

Bram stared up at him, trying to comprehend what the fuck he was talking about.

Take? He was having a panic attack. A goddamned massive, heart pounding, dizzying . . .

Take.

Drugged.

Fuck. With all the strength he could muster, he pointed to the beer he'd been handed by someone at the keg earlier.

Sweet echoed his thoughts with a decisive, "Fuck. Call the doc— Bram's been drugged."

He was restless—drowning and flying at the same time. Throat closing painfully as his leaden limbs cut through the water. But he had to get to Linc, who'd flailed and thrashed—and then his brother's head went under. Bram panicked, water filled his lungs and his cough sounded unnatural to his ears, like a death rattle.

Linc! He was yelling inside his mind. Under the water, Linc turned to look at him. Held out his hand, but then, as though an invisible force began pulling him from behind, he slowly moved away.

Bram's outstretched fingertips touched Linc's, but Bram couldn't get a grasp on them. Linc was slipping away and Bram's body tensed. He couldn't breathe. His brain clouded and then . . .

Sweet. What was Sweet doing in the water?

Bram blinked slowly, coming to, feeling the mattress under him, the realization that he was soaked from sweat. That he was nowhere near that goddamned lake. That Linc wasn't here. That Bram himself very nearly hadn't been either.

And even though he reassured himself that he wasn't drowning, he closed his eyes and went under again.

However many hours later, Bram surfaced with a deep, gasping breath of goddamned air, grasping for a body that wasn't there.

Sweet's voice broke through the roar in his ears. "Hey, you're all right. Safe."

Bram opened his mouth, but it took forever to croak out, "Felt like I never stopped moving."

"You didn't. You were looking for Linc while you were knocked out," Sweet confirmed in a voice heavy and husky from lack of sleep.

Bram blinked at him until the confusion cleared. "Shit. Was dreaming."

"I'd imagine so," Sweet said darkly. He was pissed, and it took Bram another minute to process—and recall—that none of this was his fucking fault.

"Who did this?"

"Not sure." Sweet handed him a glass of water, which Bram drank down greedily. He became aware that he was thankfully not in a hospital, but rather in Sweet's cabin. And that there was a pretty woman approaching, long blonde hair and big blue eyes. The dark-rimmed glasses she wore made her look even sexier, although Bram suspected she wore them for just the opposite reason.

"How long's he been awake?" she asked, her tone low and no-nonsense.

"Few minutes. He seems okay." Sweet vacated his seat next to Bram so she could move closer. "Bram, this is Doctor—"

"Misha," she corrected. "I'm just going to do a quick exam, okay, Bram?"

He nodded, and she listened to his chest, tested his reflexes, and asked him some standard questions.

"Great—passed with flying colors. You'll feel like crap for the next twelve hours or so before all of the drug's out of your system. Drink lots of fluids to flush it out faster, but you shouldn't have another reaction like that—you're through the worst of it," Misha told him. "But I'm around—Sweet knows how to reach me."

"Thanks." Bram noted that she hugged Sweet as she started to leave the room. "Wait—"

She turned back. "What's wrong?"

"What was it—the drug?"

"GHB." She frowned. "Apart from being affected by it, you're highly allergic to it—that's why you reacted the way you did. You started going into shock. It's not a common allergy, one you could live your whole life peacefully not knowing you had."

Bram's body chilled—utterly ice-motherfucking-cold.

"Bram, what's wrong?" Sweet asked.

One you could live your whole life peacefully not knowing you had.

But Bram *did* know.

And so did anyone who looked at his ATF records.

Because the Heathens gave him the drug after they beat him—OD'd him but it wasn't the OD that nearly killed him. It was the allergy—and the only people who knew that were the ATF agents sent by Parisi who picked him up and took him in after they discovered him.

Sweet demanded, "What is it, Bram? You got pale as a fucking ghost again."

Bram was trapped, inside his own body and inside Havoc's compound. He wasn't going to die, not from the drugging. But at the hands of Sweet and his men?

Entirely possible.

He had to tell everything, and trust that Sweet wouldn't kill him . . . or feed him to the Heathens, limb by limb.

"Bram, can you tell me how you feel?" Misha urged. "Scale of one to five, five being great."

"Two," he managed.

"Better than I expected," she said. "I'm going to run another IV to push the rest of the shit out of your system. Just lie back and try to relax."

He didn't even have the strength to laugh at her words. Instead, he let her check his vitals and he slept more, knowing he was at least safe until she was gone. Finally, he was steady enough to sit up without getting light-headed. He drank some Coke and kept it down and progressed to crackers as Misha took the IV fluids out of his arm, convinced that his health and welfare were going in the right direction.

If she had any idea of the truth, he wondered what she'd do. She'd taken an oath to do no harm. Would it matter?

Probably not, since her loyalty was to Havoc. So Bram didn't say a word to her, let his last hope walk out the door and leave him alone with Sweet, and with the truth.

Sweet, who walked slowly over to him, unshaven, handsome as fuck and looking bigger than he had earlier. Bram had been trying to wake his muscles up, testing them, flexing his hands to make sure he could fight.

Because if he could, he would.

Without any small talk, Sweet narrowed his eyes and demanded, "Who the fuck are you, Bram?"

Bram stared at him and said seriously, "I'm the guy you've been fucking."

"Not the time for your sarcastic shit. We both know it won't work."

Playing innocent for a few more minutes wouldn't either, but that didn't stop Bram from frowning slightly. "What's this all about?"

"I've got two Pagans outside who offered me the full amount of the bounty put on your head by Heathens so they can take you back and finish the job," Sweet said. Bram knew he must be a pretty damned VIP for the Pagans and the Heathens to actually work toward the same end. Then again, all the MCs were in agreement about traitors.

Sweet continued, "I'm assuming the Heathens are on their way as well. Word travels fast. I know who you are, Bram. I know you're hiding from the Heathens. There's no way out, so you need to start talking."

Under Sweet's steady stare, Bram dropped the act. "Just let me get out of here and I won't bother you again."

And then he stood up, leaving them mere inches apart, pushing his luck. As he suspected, Sweet pulled the knife he'd held in his palm and brought it up under Bram's chin. "You're a Heathen probie."

"Guess you've figured that out," Bram said evenly. "You tell me the rest of the story."

"Tell you what?" Sweet asked, an edge to his voice. "That I'm going to beat the shit out of you? Kill you? Or turn you back over to the Heathens? Because they're all viable—and called for—options."

Bram swallowed hard but didn't say anything.

Sweet continued, "Under normal circumstances, I wouldn't have even given you time to ask your question."

"So why am I still breathing?"

Sweet leaned in. "Make no mistake it's because of my generosity. Your life? In my hands."

Bram blew out a harsh breath. "What the fuck do I say to that? Thank you?"

"Be a start."

"Go fuck yourself, Sweet." His voice turned low, dangerous, the sound a caged animal would make right before it broke out and attacked. "I'm not anyone's bitch. Don't expect me to be your indentured servant, walking upright because of your good graces." Because he knew all too well how quickly those good graces could turn like the tide . . . and when that happened, it was the ugliest thing he'd ever seen.

Because he'd seen it.

His past swirled around him and he was drowning again . . . gulping water, praying, looking for help frantically . . . and seeing a man standing at the shore, staring, hands stuffed in his pockets, unwilling to help, no matter how hard Bram screamed and begged.

Parisi's assurances rang hollow in his ears. *We're coming, Bram. You can get out tonight—don't wait. Leave your apartment and don't look back.*

Bram, surrounded by Heathens. Hemmed in.

Trapped.

Betrayed.

He stared at Sweet.

Not again. Not ever again.

He'd hit the wall—his personal breaking point. In seconds, Bram had Sweet's own gun trained on him, thankful that Sweet underestimated his survival skills. "I'm walking off this compound quietly. If you want to live, I suggest you join me."

CHAPTER 13

AIN'T NO PRETTY BOY

Sweet knew Bam was strong, but he'd underestimated how fast Bram would bounce back from the drugging . . . and also underestimated that Bram would have the criminal side down pat as well, because the gun he held was Sweet's own.

And, in his other hand, Bram held Sweet's knife . . . and cell phone. Fucking pickpocket, just like his brother. "You prepared to kill me, Bram?"

Bram motioned for him to turn around without answering, and Sweet decided it was safer for everyone involved to go along quietly. Maybe the Heathens wouldn't kill Bram if Sweet was with him.

Maybe.

Bram slid cold steel cuffs around Sweet's wrists, closing them with an authoritative, definitive click.

"Is this necessary?" Sweet kept his tone purposely bored.

Bram grabbed him around the neck in a chokehold that Sweet wasn't sure he could get out of even if he hadn't been wearing cuffs. The hold was half strangulation, pure submission-forcing, and he allowed Bram to shove him forward, his steps shortened because of the hold and the gun at his carotid.

Gypsy saw them first, and then Tug and Ozzie were running over, pointing weapons of their own.

"Stand down," Sweet managed thickly. He saw other members approaching. "Don't stop him—let Bram's truck off the property."

Gypsy shook his head but Bram interjected, "I'll kill him. I've got nothing to lose. I'm a dead man either way—the only question is whether I take your boss with me."

Bram did have something to lose—Linc. But he'd sounded convincing and he was coming off the drugs. Sweet was a good judge of character, but something inside of Bram had snapped with Sweet's threats. No matter which way Sweet played this, he'd have lost.

"Stand down," Sweet ordered. "I'm going with him. That's it."

Bram shoved him into the passenger's seat of his truck, then climbed through the back seat to get to the driver's side, holding the gun on Sweet the entire time. Sweet noticed that his members had guns trained on the truck—Bram's didn't have the bulletproof windshield that Sweet's did. But Sweet shook his head and no one fired.

When he started the truck, Bram also reached over and quickly duct-taped Sweet's upper body to the back of the seat.

"Not necessary," he told Bram.

"Shut up." Bram floored the truck, nearly taking out anyone in his path. As they went down the hill, Sweet held his breath.

At times, these hills around Havoc had a mind of their own. When there was danger coming in, bikes and cars of Havoc's enemies tended to stall out for no reason at the bottom of the hill, leaving the men they carried helpless. That'd been happening since Sweet's grandfather—Finn—founded the club with three of his Army buddies, fresh out of Vietnam. Sweet always felt his grandfather's presence strongly at Havoc, like he was being looked after.

And when Bram's truck left the premises without issue, Sweet chose to take that as a sign that he'd judged Bram correctly.

Now it was time for Sweet to undo some of the damage he'd unwittingly done. "Stay off the back roads," he ordered Bram now.

"Want me to gag you?"

Sweet kept his tone mild. "Didn't know that was one of your kinks."

"Fuck off, Sweet. No blowjobs tonight."

"Are you sure? That's calmed you down before, helped you to think rationally. I'll offer up my services," Sweet said calmly as Bram kept his eyes, and full control, on speeding up the road in front of them.

Seeing Bram in action was fascinating. The man was seamless when he slid into roles, but this? This was where he shined—in control, in command.

And threatening to kill you.

But the Bram who'd spent the past days letting Sweet fuck him? That man was the real thing too. It was the guy pretending to have no direction or plan that was the fake Bram. Or were they all facets of the same man?

He was Linc's brother, so it shouldn't come as any surprise that he was as mercurial as hell. But the man next to him with a gun, an obvious case of PTSD, and a death wish promised a scenario that wasn't exactly the way Sweet had imagined this going down. "It's okay to ask for help."

"Don't talk to me like I'm a fucking mental patient," Bram snapped, then glanced at himself in the rearview. "Fine. You can. But I won't like it."

Sweet sighed. "What's your plan?"

"You shutting up."

"I'm not down with that."

"Sweet, I'm going to have to kill some Heathens before they kill me. I'm sure MCs other than Pagans will have a bounty on my head. The faster I move away from Havoc, the less reasons the Heathens have to suspect that you conspired with me. So my plan is to keep alive long enough to find Linc."

It all made sense—Bram's aversion to his rocker that first night, and to the bar and the compound in general.

Shit. Sweet could definitely understand that, because he knew how the Heathens operated. They treated their members the same way they treated their enemies. And when Sweet had threatened him . . . "Bram, I can help."

Bram snorted. "I've got all the help I can manage."

"You can't win this."

"You think I don't know that?" he exploded. "The fuck, Sweet? You think I'm that goddamned stupid? Least I can do is get you off the hook for my shit. I didn't want to bring that onto Havoc. I just want to find Linc—that's it. That's all. But you pushed—wouldn't let me leave. What did you expect me to do—fight you and the Heathens at the same time?"

"No, I didn't. But I didn't know about that until now." Sweet paused. "You say it's about finding Linc . . . but what about you, Bram? What's going to happen to you if you leave?"

"I'm dead," he said flatly, with a bluntness that made even Sweet's hardened nerves startle. "That's how this shakes out. All of this is just prolonging the inevitable. Prolonging it enough to find Linc."

"That's bullshit. You wouldn't have made it this far if you really believed that."

"Thanks for the psychoanalysis. The psycho part's fitting."

"You don't know the half of it," Sweet said darkly.

"I know more than half."

"You know about the Heathens. How they run their shit. Don't even pretend that my club's anything like that shithole."

"Right. You're just 'clubs.' All protective and shit. Wanting to live out your days the way you want to, without outside involvement."

"We police our own. We stay out of the town's business except to contribute to their economy and keep them safe, yes. And you? You're protected, right?"

Bram didn't answer that, just said, "Shut the fuck up."

"I don't do that for anyone," Sweet shot back. Because he wanted to see just how far he could push this. "And why'd you get involved with the Heathens in the first place? Plenty of other clubs would've been happy to have you."

Bram laughed darkly. "Little late for that now." He paused. "A friend from the Army said there were like minds there. A place I should look into. I worked so much, never stayed in one place. I thought a connection—any connection—might help." The truth of the last sentences caught audibly, bitterly in his throat.

"Guess that backfired."

"You have no idea."

It was only then that the pieces began to connect for Sweet. They should have immediately, but the intel had come at him, fast and furious. The drugging and the accusations, being dragged out of Havoc at gunpoint . . .

Bram.

Heathens.

Beating. "They did that to you," Sweet said. "The scars. The anxiety around MCs."

Bram didn't answer. Didn't need to. His silence, coupled with the tension radiating off his body, told Sweet the truth of his statements.

"Dammit." Sweet put his head back against the headrest as Bram's truck hurtled down the highway. "Now it all makes sense. Fucking comparing us to Heathens. Thinking we'd kill you any second."

Bram laughed darkly. "Prove me wrong yet?"

"I could ask you the same thing."

"As long as we're trading truths, why don't you tell me what Linc really did, besides jumping bail?"

"He took out credit cards in Gypsy's name, right before he got arrested the third time. Gypsy got notice of the credit card fraud."

Bram nodded tightly. "Did you ask Linc about it?"

"No, we were just keeping him close. Keeping an eye on him."

Bram glanced at him. "And we all know how well your protection works out, don't we?"

Bram exhaled, fought to remain calm and rational. He needed to get Sweet to a safe spot, get him the hell out of the truck and then . . .

And then . . . "When were you going to tell me about Linc and the credit card shit?"

"I wasn't."

"So that's another reason I'm here. You're watching out for all your money, waiting for me to bring Linc back to you. You're going to fuck with my brother and make me betray him to you."

Sweet didn't deny it, because he couldn't. Bram wasn't sure if he was more pissed at himself for getting suckered in or at Sweet, who put himself out there as an awesome family guy. "You know the fraud is bullshit. He was set up," Bram snapped.

"You know he's an admitted thief."

Bram was already shaking his head. "He wouldn't steal—not from Rush. Not from friends, which I'm guessing he thought Gypsy was—and Havoc too."

"Then stay with Havoc and we'll find him together and sort this out," Sweet said reasonably.

"Guess what? No matter how much you talk to me like I'm a fucking mental patient, I'm not finding Linc for you."

"Not much I can do to challenge that right now, except find Linc myself," Sweet reasoned.

"I'm going to pull over soon. I'll call Gypsy and tell him where I'm leaving you. Then you're getting the fuck out of this truck."

"Come back to Havoc with me. Please, Bram."

If he didn't lie to Sweet, make Sweet hate him, Sweet would attempt to save him—maybe because he truly wanted to but mainly in order to get his hands on Linc. That wasn't happening. "I'm a dead man walking. I took advantage of you and your club."

Sweet's expression hardened. "Let me help you."

"Why? So you can kill me afterwards?"

"Is that what you think?"

"We've known each other for what, less than a week. What should I expect?"

Sweet stared at him. "You should expect everything, Bram. Sometimes it takes forever. Sometimes you know in twenty-four hours."

Bram felt like a hand had literally reached into his chest and squeezed his heart. But he knew that it was only a matter of time before he heard Harleys revving up, loud engines, roaring on their way to catch him. But his truck was equipped, thanks to his undercover job on an illegal racetrack, to give him the extra speed to lose the bikes. Plus, he'd always been good at evade and escape, so this panicked race was really in his mind more so than on the road.

Still, he was outnumbered. They would circle him and eventually catch up, especially if he stayed in town. And having Sweet next to him? Helped at first but now was a definite liability.

At that point, the chances of finding Linc alive . . .

Fuck it. He yanked the wheel into a parking lot, even though he had to cross two lanes to do it.

"Didn't know stunt driver was a part of your résumé," Sweet said wryly, seemingly unperturbed by his stint as a hostage.

Because he was a damned good actor. "You only want Linc back in order to punish him. Now get the fuck out."

"Bram—"

"No. No more explaining or psychoanalyzing. Get out now or I'll knock you out and throw you out of the damned car."

"I think you should consider other options."

Right. Like confessing I'm ATF. "I'm out of options." Bram unlocked the doors as he pulled his weapon.

"You wouldn't."

Bram fired, the bullet whizzing past Sweet into a telephone pole. "I wouldn't shoot? Try me again."

When Sweet didn't move, Bram shot again, and this time, blood blossomed along Sweet's forearm.

"You motherfucker."

"Out," Bram ordered, and Sweet listened this time. Bram took off with the passenger's door still open, using a wide turn to slam it shut. And he didn't look back once in the rearview.

Looking back would do nothing. And that's what he was left with. Nothing. Just like he'd had before.

And the shit was about to hit the fan. The dark vibrations of angry motorcycles trailed him nightly in his dreams, but this? This was no dream. In his rearview, he could now see the clear line of single headlights on his six.

Foes, not friends. Up ahead, a Heathen-made roadblock.

They don't know you're ATF.

But he wasn't sure if that was better or worse. At this point, it probably didn't matter either way—the beating he'd endure this time would hurt just the same. And whoever it was who turned him in— Sweet or Gypsy or Tug—didn't matter.

Granted, if it had been Sweet . . .

Ah, fuck it. He'd always known he couldn't trust anyone anyway, should've stuck to his own rules and gotten the hell out of Shades and Havoc as soon as he realized what Linc had done.

He glanced in the rearview, feeling his body calm down, the way it needed to in situations like this. Panic would get him nowhere.

He dialed his phone without looking. "Dozer, listen—they know."

"Know what?"

"Where I am. Literally. They're tailing me." Another glance in the rearview confirmed it, but his heartbeat had slowed and his foot pressed the gas into the floor.

Dozer cursed. "Bram, I never—"

"I know, man. Not why I'm calling." He jerked the car hard and fast, off-road. Defensive driving was something he could do in his sleep. Losing the tail wasn't the problem—it was what happened when the next tail found him. "I'm just calling to tell you, so you know . . ."

"No way, Bram—not like this. I'll send in backup."

Bram shook his head, like Doz was sitting next to him to see it. "No, you can't."

"Bram—" Dozer managed to sound calm, not desperate, which helped.

"Just listen. If I don't come out of this, you'd need to find Linc."

"What the fuck."

"Sorry to put this on you."

Dozer's anger sizzled through the phone. "Don't you fucking act like you're dying on my watch. No way, Bram, because I plan on strangling you myself for putting yourself in danger. So plan to stay alive long enough for my hands to go around your throat," Dozer threatened, and for the first time that night, Bram actually laughed.

And planned. The radio was on low, mainly to soothe his jangled nerves, to turn him back into that soldier he once was. He slipped on that persona like a well-loved, well-worn overcoat, an armor, a layer of protection.

Yeah, he was going to go fuck some shit up.

CHAPTER 14

VOICES IN THE SKY

Twenty minutes later, Ozzie was escorting Sweet into the truck parked outside the diner. There was a second truck parked behind it and for now, all four men got into one of them as they discussed their next moves.

"What the hell happened?" Ozzie demanded when Sweet clicked on the overhead light and began digging through the glove compartment for gauze.

"It's just a graze," Sweet muttered. Burned like hell, the same way the anger did. He wasn't sure who he was angrier at—Bram or himself. "I'm fine. Bram's not."

Tug let out a low growl but didn't say anything. He was busy keeping eyes out for both trucks, because tonight they were too vulnerable for bikes. Half of Havoc was guarding Havoc and the others were out on the road, looking for Heathens and ready to back Sweet up.

"Who gives a fuck if Bram's not fine. He used the club," Gypsy said angrily.

He used you was the bigger, unspoken allegation, but Sweet ignored the sentiment. Whether it was because he didn't buy it or because he didn't want to believe it, he wasn't sure. Both he and Bram had betrayed each other. There wasn't time to argue about which was worse. "We're not handing him over to the Heathens."

"Bram's one of them," Tug said.

But Sweet couldn't get a handle on that supposed truth—it didn't connect or make sense. He'd met Heathens, grown up near enough of them to learn their mindset. The ones who didn't belong stuck out like sore thumbs, and they tended to get out quickly—often painfully, as was the case for several ex-members who Havoc actually respected.

Sweet could call on them now to investigate this shit further, or he could go with his gut, since that's what got him through wars, on this soil with the MC and overseas with the Army. It's what put him in the position to run Havoc.

He hadn't risen to leadership by being indecisive. He wasn't about to change that now. "We're getting Bram back. He stays at Havoc. We get Linc back. Prepare to deal with those consequences."

Gypsy shook his head slowly. "Sweet—"

"Since when do we let anyone tell us what to do?" he demanded.

"When a Heathen is—"

"Asking for our protection," Sweet finished. "Doesn't seem like he wants to be a Heathen anymore, right?"

"He was a part of them for two years," Tug pointed out, while Ozzie remained quiet, watching and waiting.

"Isn't that enough time to learn a lesson?" Sweet growled. "Everyone makes mistakes."

Before anyone could answer, Sweet's phone began to ring, a number he didn't recognize. Tonight, he answered anyway. "Who's this?"

"Friend of Bram's. Is this Sweet?"

"How do I know who the fuck you are?" Sweet asked.

"I know he took you out of Havoc and left you at the diner on Route 6. Tied you to the seat. I know you left him your knife and gun. How's that?"

That, for now, bought the man on the other end of the phone validity. "Your name."

"Dozer. Want to know where Bram is or not? Because if you're not going to help him, I swear to fuck I'll come there and take you apart."

Dozer's tone was fierce. Sweet wanted to hang up but he forced himself to say, "We'll take him to safety."

"He's headed east on route 6, with Heathens on his ass."

"Can you be more specific about location?" Sweet asked.

"Start driving and I'll keep talking," was Dozer's answer.

Three hours later, Bram had taken the Heathens following him on a wild ride, lost them (and made sure three bikes went down into a ditch off the side of the road) and now he was holed up in a safe house Dozer had pointed him to. It was really just a hunting shack in the middle of nowhere, but it had running water and electricity.

He worked best in the dark, preparing dozens of incendiary devices that would blow when he called the Heathens and led them this way. He'd head out the back of the shack as the night blew the fuck up. From there? Who knew.

Maybe he'd invade the Heathens compound—the Pagans too—to see if Linc was really and truly there. If he wasn't . . .

If he wasn't, Bram was going to have to move along and save himself. And he resigned himself to that fact as the storm that'd been threatening all night rolled in, fast and furious. It would be over within the hour, so he settled himself into the cot in the meantime, to lie there in the dark and think about his options like he was a boy who'd gotten himself in trouble in school and needed to sit in the corner.

Except back then, he didn't have an entire life to rethink. Contemplating shit these days wasn't for the weak. He hadn't been perfect but his mistakes had been few and far between. He'd made his choices. The only thing he regretted was not trying harder with Linc, but hell, that wasn't exactly under his control. Linc had a mind of his own.

"Dammit, Linc—where the hell are you?" he asked out loud into the darkness and tried to imagine Linc's future . . . and his own.

What future? Because Bram wasn't going to hang out at a biker compound for the rest of his life.

But you're not going back to the ATF either, are you?

Granted, he could go back and fight for justice, for him and for other men Parisi screwed over, no doubt for the all-fucking-mighty dollar. Bram was sure he wasn't the first, and he could try to make sure he was the last, on Parisi's watch anyway. And maybe he'd do that, but then what—stick around and ride a desk? Keep doing undercover work until he was old and gray?

Bram's hand shook, mainly pain and some withdrawal, and he searched his pockets in hope there was something there to smooth the rough spots.

Just a pack of cigarettes—and hell, better than nothing. He ignored the amount of time it took him to light the damned thing. Thanked his lucky stars he'd wired the place before this shit started.

In the back of his mind, he was aware of the fact that this place could blow with him in it. That even if he tried to escape out the back at the perfect time, everything could catch too soon, trapping him. He'd placed the explosives precisely, but that didn't mean they'd behave as such. They were as unpredictable as humans.

He knew it. Should be waiting in the woods behind this shack but no, he was tempting fate by lying on the cot, starting at the ceiling, watching smoke curl like it was trying to touch Heaven.

Good fucking luck. That was the closest he was getting.

CHAPTER 15

HELLRAISER

Dozer gave him Bram's phone number, and Sweet hesitated before dialing, not wanting to drive him even further away. But he risked it . . . and wasn't surprised when Bram actually picked up.

"Do you need rescuing?" was Bram's first question.

Confident fucker. "I was going to ask you the same thing."

"I'm good. Just stay at Havoc."

"Too late."

"Ah, come on. You don't get it, Sweet," Bram said tiredly.

"Then tell me." Sweet kept the phone to his ear as Tug drove the cage in the darkness. He hated the claustrophobia of the vehicle, but it was a necessary evil to bypass Heathens safely.

"All I want to do is find Linc. End of story."

"You can't do that alone."

"Bullshit I can't."

Sweet sighed. "You need to let Havoc help you."

At that, Bram snorted. "Right. I fucking kidnapped you. I lied to you. You want my balls, the same way Heathens does—and I get it. You've got your club rules. I knew them and I broke them. I'm a big boy, Sweet. And I pay my own dues."

Bram hung up the phone. He'd sounded so goddamned calm and determined, a man prepared to go out with a bang.

If Sweet knew him—and he figured that he did—Bram had booby-trapped his hiding spot to take as many Heathens to hell as he could. And then some.

That made things all the more complicated for this rescue. If Linc were here, Sweet could pick his brain, find out how Bram's mind worked.

But Linc wasn't . . . and Sweet needed to trust himself that he did indeed know how Bram's mind worked.

He leaned his head back against the seat and closed his eyes for a long moment.

When he opened them, he dialed Vann's number.

"Vann? You sure he called Vann?" Gypsy asked when the trucks were parked at the bottom of the long hill, a mile from the shack Bram was holed up in.

"He called Vann," Tug confirmed.

"I called Vann," Sweet said to stop the bullshit game of WTF telephone currently happening right in front of his motherfucking face.

"Feeling suicidal?" Gypsy asked.

"No, but I'm guessing you are," Sweet shot back.

Gypsy looked completely unworried about Sweet's warning, but Sweet knew Gypsy would back him. And when Vann—a rogue member of Havoc MC who Sweet called in for very special occasions—rounded the corner silently and had probably been standing there listening to them say his name for the past five minutes, all Gypsy said was, "I told you he was a fuckin' lunatic."

"Obviously you're in need of a fucking lunatic, so it's a good thing I was free tonight." Vann's eyes seemed to glow in the moonlight, an almost unnatural amber color that threw both friends and enemies off. They made him look crazy. Unbalanced.

Of course, he was, so the eyes had it. Sweet cut directly to the chase. "Got a former military guy ready to go down with the ship—and take a whole boatload of Heathens with him."

"You want me to take out the traps so you can save the Heathens?" Vann asked.

Asshole knew exactly what Sweet was asking, so he wrapped his hand around Vann's throat and murmured, "Fucking with me now's a bad idea. You're alive because of my goodwill. Don't forget it."

Vann's eyes stared through him. When Sweet eased off, Vann said, "I'll get your boy out."

"Then go."

"Need help?" Tug asked. He and Vann had worked together once before—successfully, since Tug was still alive. Vann gave a nod and he and Tug disappeared into the darkness.

"Now that's a team from hell," Gypsy remarked.

"And night's like these are exactly why you need that."

"Guy knows what he's doing. Wouldn't mind meeting him," Vann said three hours later as all the men converged together by the road, half a mile from where Bram was still holed up. No one else had come by—other Havoc members were busy throwing Heathens off the trail and protecting the compound.

Sweet crossed his arms. "You sure it's cleaned up?"

"Sure. I'm guessing you want to take him and then have me rerig everything."

"Yeah. Need me to leave Tug with you?"

Vann gave a hard shake of his head but clapped Tug on the shoulder. "Nope. Dismantling's the hard part. I can fix it back in a third of the time. And I'll wait around to watch the bodies blow."

"Good. I'll go in alone. Tug, keep watch. I'll call you in first if things go bad."

Tug nodded silently.

Vann offered, "You should make sure this guy doesn't shoot you again, though. Unless that's foreplay to you," with a smile.

"Get the fuck out of my face, Vann," Sweet snarled.

Vann snorted but complied, and Sweet marched determinedly along the path that Vann and Tug had just walked, climbing the steep hill up to the safe house that Bram had made his own.

It was a simple hunting shack that had been in these parts forever. But Sweet bet it had never been used as a death trap.

IRON FIST

Surrounded. Taken down. At first, he fought, but there were far too many of them, armed with pipes and chains, and he concentrated on curling into a ball when the pain got too fierce, trying to protect his head from the swift kick coming his way . . .

Shit. Bram shook his head in the darkness of the woods he'd finally walked out into. Now wasn't the time for a flashback of his beating—that could easily bring on a panic attack. Now was the time to watch Heathens blow the fuck up. And judging by the sounds of bikes coming closer, that would happen soon.

He smoked cigarette after cigarette in an effort to forget the pain inhabiting every inch of his body. Because working through it was getting him a step closer to Linc.

He'd head to the Heathens clubhouse after this. It wasn't like he thought Linc was being held there. No, the Heathens had plenty of places they held the people they kidnapped—and Bram hadn't been privy to any of those. But storming the clubhouse when the Heathens were in a time of confusion might get him somewhere . . .

Like possibly dead. But a plan was a plan. He was moving forward. Better to burn out than fade away and all that shit.

He stared out into the darkness, and then, after several more minutes, he froze as the hairs on the back of his neck stood on end. Because he suddenly knew that he wasn't alone out here. "I told you not to come."

"I don't take orders from anyone," was Sweet's response.

Bram turned to look directly into Sweet's eyes, and there was no way the guy could've gotten in here, never mind up the hill, without being blown to fucking pieces. "Did you fuck with my traps?"

"Yes. And now they're reset." As Sweet spoke, the sound of bikes grew closer.

"Is that Havoc?"

"Havoc is safely tucked away, ready to watch the fireworks."

"You're not taking credit for it," Bram said tightly.

"Yeah, we are, or you're not living long enough to find your brother."

Those were the last words Bram heard before the area thirty feet from them began to blow to high hell, and he stared, mesmerized by the hot flames that came just close enough to remind him that he'd taken down some evil bastards.

With pleasure. Burn now, burn forever.

Who's the dead man walking now?

You still are, he reminded himself as the flames began to burn out. Soon the death toll would be exposed, the familiar sirens would blare, and he had to move before the police got here.

"You're going to come with me, Bram."

It was then that Bram realized Sweet had taken his gun and knife off him while he'd been caught up in watching the explosions.

"We've proven that we can each overpower the other, given the right circumstances," Sweet started. "So given that we're equally matched, maybe calling a truce and dealing with this shit together makes sense."

Bram groaned inwardly, his head throbbing. Because yeah, he could overpower Sweet, but he couldn't handle another chase tonight. Not with the police. "Fuck."

"I'll take that as a yes," Sweet added.

"How'd you find me?"

Sweet shrugged. "You've got your secrets, I've got mine."

Bram was about to say, *You know mine*, but Sweet didn't. Not really. Not all. "I want to go to Heathens clubhouse."

"You're not going anywhere."

"Sweet—"

"Bram, I have men there, checking things out. If they find anything—"

"I don't trust Havoc," Bram bit out.

"I know that. But you have to—for Linc's sake."

"Load of bullshit," Bram muttered, but he still let Sweet lead him through the woods in the dark and into a small clearing where a van waited for them. Filled with friendly Havoc members, he thought wryly, but to his surprise, the van was empty.

He got into the passenger's seat and let Sweet drive them away from the wreckage.

It was a mistake. He knew it and he'd still gotten into the truck because the choices facing him were equally deadly. It was the choice of who he'd rather kill him, Havoc or Heathens.

Havoc might show some mercy, if for no other reason than Linc and Rush. Then again, dead was dead.

"We're going to take the long was around," Sweet told him. "Head through a drive-through for an alibi."

"I'm guessing they'll fix the time stamp," Bram said and got a curt nod in response. "And then where're you taking me?"

Sweet frowned like he was crazy to ask that question. "Back to Havoc."

Bram barely had the strength to glare at him. "You've got to be fucking kidding me, right? First, there's the small matter of someone in your club trying to kill me with a roofie—"

"It wasn't Havoc."

"How convenient," Bram said dryly. "Still, I kidnapped Havoc's president, I'm a former Heathen probie, and I'm going to waltz back in there for Havoc to keep me safe."

"You're looking at Havoc," Sweet reminded him. "And it was noted that you saved me."

"I shot you."

Sweet pulled over to the side of the road and focused on Bram. "Grazed. And it's not the best time to remind me, unless you really do want to die."

Bram leaned in across the middle partition and paused before he put a light finger on the base of Sweet's throat. "Remember—we're only equal because of those fucking drugs. Otherwise . . ."

"I could take you without blinking," Sweet growled.

Bram gave him a slight smile. "Keep on believing that, okay?" And then he cupped the back of Sweet's neck and yanked him in for a hard kiss before settling back into his seat.

Sweet put the car into gear and they drove in silence for a while, until they drove through the fast food window and ordered. Bram didn't want to eat but he knew he had to. Wished for the thousandth time he had pain pills on him.

"You're hurting," Sweet said as they got back onto the road and Bram dug into the bag of food.

"We've all got our problems."

Sweet gave a stuttered laugh. "And yours is being unable to accept help."

Because you don't know anything about me. Because I'm so fucked up. Because I'm the law, and when you find out, you'll hate me and kill me, maybe not in that order.

Bram swallowed hard. "By help, you're talking protection. Havoc's protection. And I've already had a taste of what that entails."

"I don't give a shit. Your choices are in my hands now," Sweet told him. "Now, tell me about your friend."

Bram's stomach tightened. "Who's that?"

"The one who told me where you were. How'd you meet? I'm guessing he was Army too."

Yeah, Sweet's tone was too fucking sarcastically innocent, and Bram thought briefly about taking the wheel from Sweet and running them off the road . . . but he assumed that Sweet was being tailed by other Havoc members. "Yes."

"That all?"

"He's got my back."

"Right. He a Heathen too? Or are you both just spies for them?"

Shit. Having Sweet think he was a spy for the Heathens was marginally worse than admitting he was ATF. He ran his options. He could overpower Sweet, who'd made a tactically stupid decision to drive and have Bram alone with him in the truck. But escape wouldn't be easy. And killing Sweet? Not on his to-do list. It made him ache to just think about it . . . and it worried him that he felt that way. "I've got to tell you something."

Sweet nodded, like he'd expected this. Then he pulled off road, and Bram watched the bikes he'd suspected were there come into view and circle back to guard them. "They're quiet—you guys have different kinds of bikes?"

Sweet shrugged. "Sometimes stealth is required. I'm guessing you know all about that. Now go ahead, Bram. Tell me about the Heathens. Tell me how they put you up to this. Tell me about how you, your friend, and your brother have been playing us."

"No, we haven't. My friend and Linc have nothing to do with the Heathens."

"So it's just you."

"Sweet, I'm undercover ATF." The words came out in an easy rush and relief swept him. No more secrets.

No more cover.

Most likely, no more breathing either.

"You're either truly motherfucking stupid or you think I am," Sweet growled, and this time, Bram accepted the gun to his head with all the grace his exhaustion would allow.

Because death wish. "Neither."

"I don't believe this shit."

"I didn't come here for anything or anyone except Linc. That's my only goddamned interest."

"Right. I'll believe you because you've been so truthful."

"And if I'd shared this up front? What? You'd have treated me worse than the Heathens did. And maybe Linc too."

"Is Linc ATF too?" Sweet demanded.

"No. Former Army but definitely not a fed."

"Not a snitch working for a fed?" Sweet asked. "Maybe you and Linc planned this so you could come in and cozy up."

"I've been trying to fucking leave so I don't pull Havoc into anything."

Sweet cocked the hammer on his gun, the sound echoing in Bram's ears. "Too. Fucking. Late."

As Sweet continued to hold the gun to Bram's skull, Bram's chin lifted—defiance and pride and not an ounce of goddamned fear Sweet could see.

Not an ounce of common sense, either. "It's been too late for me since the Heathens nearly killed me. I'm dead either way."

Sweet should just shoot him, or take him back to the Heathens, guilt-free. Fuck the bounty. He'd never take scum money. But there was something about Bram . . . and there was definitely more to this story. "Start talking."

"I was an undercover with the Heathens for two years. I was a probie."

"With a death wish," Sweet muttered.

"Maybe," Bram admitted. "I could've turned the job down, but I was a good fit. No family besides grown siblings. Military background. I'd just come off another big undercover job. I was good at getting in. Heathens liked the way I fought. I saved their road manager and some of the others from getting arrested. Right place, right time."

Sweet didn't believe that last part, but it didn't matter. "Did you ever do anything against Havoc for the Heathens or the ATF?"

"No. Neither group wants contact with you. That's what I was told."

Which was pure truth. Havoc was like the elite special ops of the MC world. Going up against them was futile. They weren't angels, but their ventures were (mostly) legal and nonviolent. They were insular. But disrespect Havoc and all hellfire would rain down on the offender. Havoc believed in swift, nonnegotiable retribution. They'd also never been convicted. "Something obviously went bad."

"I gave the ATF—my sup, specifically—a lot of intel about the club and their meth trade. I helped shut things down before they started. Vipers MC helped get things started against the Heathens, and that's when I went in, but I was able to give additional information to cripple more of their drug operation." He paused, because Havoc knew and respected Vipers. "They'd also been working with two FBI agents who'd clear them of wrongdoing."

"And you turned those men in too."

"Yes."

Sweet sighed internally and lowered his weapon carefully. He moved away from Bram to stop him from attempting to grab the gun. "Do they know?"

Bram shrugged. "I don't know. Or I didn't think so, but after this . . . look, my sup told me to lay low after I got out."

"And before that? What went wrong?"

Bram cleared his throat. "It was the night before my official patch-in. I was going to disappear, because I knew they wouldn't let me walk. But it was a setup. They were waiting for me. They beat the shit out of me. They found out I was planning on leaving. Fuck, I didn't know at the time how they knew—I didn't tell anyone but Parisi. He knew it was my last night with the Heathens. I partied as usual. Made plans to ride with the guys the next day. Went back to my apartment. I was going to leave most of the shit there, since it was a safe house and it's not like I wanted any Heathen souvenirs." Bram took a deep breath, and Sweet could see that he was starting to relive that night.

"But Parisi let the Heathens know your plans."

"That's the only way they'd know . . ." Bram trailed off, ran a hand through his hair. "I was leaving out the back. I was leaving the bike behind too, figured maybe the guys would think I was killed or something. I got halfway up the block and they pulled me into an alley."

Premeditated. When Sweet got his hands on Parisi—and he would—he'd mete out his own brand of justice. "What did you tell them?"

"That I was taking a walk, to clear my head." Bram laughed. They must've had good reason not to believe him. "I'd even thought for a fleeting second that they were going to patch me in as a surprise." He shook his head. "I don't want to talk about this."

"You have to."

Bram shook his head but ground out, "They said they knew I was leaving. I denied it. Told them, 'What kind of idiot just leaves everything behind?' They told me they knew I was going to fake my own death because I didn't want to be a Heathen. That I was a betrayal to the club. That since I wanted to be a dead man so badly, they'd help me along."

"You almost died."

Bram nodded. "They know I'm still breathing. I look different, can't be easily made, but according to Dozer, they know where I am. They don't know I'm ATF, but they've been put on my tail."

"Who did that, Bram?"

Bram stared him down. "I told you—it was my sup. Dozer's my ATF connection—my only one. He wasn't on the case, but he confirmed that my sup set me up."

"So the Heathens know you're ATF?"

"No. Not yet, anyway." Bram looked away. "As far as they know, I'm just a probie they want dead to avenge their honor. I guess my sup figures dead is dead, so why get his hands—and the ATF's—dirty. Besides, he'd have to admit that he put me in there. It's easier for Parisi if I get killed because they thought I was a rat. The way I figure it, all the work I did goes to shit, the Heathens—and Parisi—don't lose any money."

It was an unbelievable story in some ways . . . but Bram wasn't the first to infiltrate an MC. He had the scars to prove the near-death beatdown, confirmed by word on the street and the bounty on his head. "Christ, Bram."

"Someone at Havoc drugged me purposely," Bram told him.

"You're already on thin ice—"

"And so is Havoc. You've got someone undercover on your payroll, or else you've got a Heathen in there. One who knows my sup."

"And you know this how?"

"My files aren't open access. I'm classified. Very few people know who I am. Only one has access to my medical records, beyond my doctors. My sup knows I'm allergic to HGB. So did the Heathens. They gave it to me the night they beat me."

"We've got a big problem here," Sweet said, his voice grim.

"I know. Look, it can end here. At least your involvement. They'll leave Havoc alone if I'm gone, Heathens and ATF."

"And you'll go where?"

"Don't worry about it."

Why Sweet did wasn't a mystery. "I have to." He started the truck and pulled back onto the road.

"What the fuck, Sweet? You can't take me back to Havoc. Not now."

"Especially now. I've got to check your story out."

"And get me killed in the process? Just fucking shoot me and get it over with. And let's not pretend I'm the criminal here."

"I do what I need to so my club—my people—stay safe," Sweet told him, his voice steady.

"So you take the law into your own hands."

"With my kind of people? Yes."

"Your kind of people?"

"MCs deal with the rules of the road. The law can't police the clubs as effectively as we police ourselves. It's road justice. It keeps everyone honest and the community safe."

"Because MCs don't do anything illegal, right?"

A muscle in Sweet's jaw jumped. "My club doesn't hurt women or children. We don't hurt anyone who doesn't deserve it. MCs are made up of big boys—we all know what we're getting into. It's business. And I don't need to justify any of this to you." Sweet paused. "Unless you're planning on taking me down?"

Sweet glanced over, saw Bram's hands tightened into fists on his thighs. "That's not why this all started."

"If it ends that way, I'll end you."

The threat hung between them, the heaviest of weights neither man could ignore. "Havoc wasn't part of my territory."

"You posed as an MC member. Doesn't matter that it was for a dirty club."

"Right. I deserve to die."

"You're a snitch."

That Sweet would even consider calling him that . . . fuck. Bram fought the urge to grab the wheel, crash them both into a ditch and beat the hell out of him.

Instead, he ground out, "Trying to take down a meth ring makes me a snitch? Then that's exactly what I fucking am."

There was no way to resolve this, not without blood and bullets. Bram had already dragged Havoc too far into it. Now he had to put some distance between himself and Sweet and hope his skills could come out and play before his PTSD did.

"Are you trying to force me to kill you?" Sweet asked. "You're not getting off that easy."

"Never do."

"Maybe it's because you hang with the wrong group of people."

"Must be nice to have the perfect brotherhood," Bram practically spat, suddenly completely angry—unreasonably so—at Sweet. "Keep them in line by threat of death and everyone pretends they love you."

"Threats don't work—promises do," Sweet intoned. "And yes, we run our club differently, but of course there are betrayals. They're unexpected and they suck, but they're dealt with swiftly. And by the whole club."

"Yeah, I know the drill, Sweet." Bram barely choked the words out. "I know what it's like to be dealt with swiftly by the whole fucking club."

Sweet paused. "How much of this—us—was a cover?"

Us. Did Sweet think there was an *us* at all? That made Bram's throat tighten, because he'd assumed he was just a fuck to Sweet, nothing more. "Guess I could ask you the same fucking question and probably get the same goddamned answer. You do what you need to for your club brothers and I do it for mine."

Sweet's eyes went cold.

Way to play your role, Bram. Way to play your role.

It truly was the only thing he did well. He didn't see that changing anytime soon.

CHAPTER 17

YOU AIN'T GOT A HOLD ON ME

The ride back to Havoc was long and tense, maybe more so for Bram than Sweet. Or maybe the MC pres was a damned good poker player.

Once back on the compound, the chances of Bram escaping were pretty much null, at least not with ten men surrounding him plus a hundred more placed around to secure perimeters.

"Quite a military operation you've got here," Bram said as he was ushered inside the clubhouse and into Sweet's office.

"Trying to get intel?" Sweet smiled and shut the door behind him, leaving just the two of them.

"You like to live dangerously, don't you?" Bram glanced at the window and then back at Sweet.

"You want to kill me, go ahead. You've had a shitload of opportunity and yet I'm still breathing." Sweet crossed his arms. "During your most recent undercover job, did you kill anyone?"

Bram gazed at him. "Got a wire in that vest? Looking to sell me out to my own people?"

"I'll take that as a yes." Sweet tapped his fist lightly against the desk.

"What about you, Sweet? How many people have you killed?"

"Like I told you, we take care of our own or mete out our own kind of justice. We're judge, jury, and executioner." Sweet's expression was defiant, his tone daring Bram to question it.

"Can't judge you, Sweet," Bram admitted. "I just know that shit like that changes you."

"Then maybe I needed changing," Sweet said unapologetically. "We're having church in a few. Tug and Ozzie will take you to the basement. Do I need to call in other guys for that?"

Did he? Bram hadn't made up his mind as to whether or not he was going to go nuts and blow Sweet's trust . . . or if he'd just cooperate. For now. "I'm fine with those two."

Sweet motioned for him to turn around. When he did, Sweet slid the cold metal cuffs on him, and being restrained was way less exciting than it had been in bed. "These have been specially soldered. You'll have a hell of a time getting out of them. Save your bones and don't bother."

Bram nodded, his body taut. Ozzie came into the office and put a light hand on his biceps to lead him, and Tug followed behind, neither man saying a word or making eye contact.

The basement was a typical cement-and-cinderblock dark, dank space, fitted with two cells, Havoc's own version of a drunk tank. The bars were sturdy, no windows in the cells and yeah, Bram was going nowhere fast.

Granted, he could've taken the keys from Ozzie's pocket easily enough. Thought about it but the way out was up. Through Havoc.

Dead man walking.

Sweet gathered Gypsy, Tug, Ozzie, and Boomer around the table. These men knew Linc well, and they'd known Bram for the short time he'd been there. But this wasn't going to be an easy church.

"I've got news—about Bram," Sweet started. "I still want to verify a few things, but in the ride over here, Bram admitted that he was ATF."

Dead silence met his statement. He took advantage of that to push forward. "He was working to take down the Heathens. Says he was betrayed by his supervisor. The beating he took? Heathens."

Tug whistled softly under his breath. "Do the Heathens know?"

"Bram says they don't. And I'd rather they never did. This is complicated enough."

"Sweet, what the fuck is he still doing here? He's ATF," Gypsy said. Slowly. Deliberately.

"He's Linc's brother."

"He's ATF," Gypsy growled. "And now he's inside Havoc—"

"It's not like he's gotten any inside information."

"He's the law, Sweet."

"He's Linc's brother," Sweet said firmly. "Don't ignore my instincts."

Bram counted four hours, twenty-three minutes, and forty-five seconds before the shaking got too bad. Fucking pain pills. Fucking withdrawal.

After rounding off another couple of hours, he was a sweating, shaking mess. He was also half-dreaming, half-hallucinating. Hearing things. Motorcycles. Chains.

Heathens, surrounding him. He tried to stand and fell, and he was surrounded. He heard himself yelling, but they were pulling him farther into the alley . . .

"Leave him alone. Stay back." Sweet's voice. What was Sweet doing here? "Bram, it's okay. You're all right."

Bram blinked up at him. *So far from it, man, you have no idea.*

"No one's going to hurt you."

Bram couldn't help it. He laughed, a crazy, uncontrolled sound. And he lay there, on the floor, with no one touching him, beating him, or threatening to kill him. But the day was still young.

Sweet called his sister, and Misha was at Havoc within half an hour. She found Sweet half holding Bram, mainly to keep him from hurting himself. Bram, of course, fought the hold, but he was shaking badly.

"When's the last time he took anything?" Misha asked.

"He was gone for at least twelve hours—his pill bottle was still in his bag." Sweet motioned to the table where Ozzie had brought in and left Bram's prescriptions. "He's been back here for a while."

Misha glanced at the bottles, opened them, and nodded before giving Bram her attention again. They tied him down so she could get a needle in his arm, but she assured him, "I'll untie you as soon as the meds start working, okay?"

"No more of that shit," Bram mumbled.

"Slow and steady. Give me seventy-two hours and you'll feel a hell of a lot better than if you go cold turkey," Misha told him.

"I didn't think he was an addict," Sweet said after she'd gotten the IV successfully going and began to untie his arms. He almost stopped her, but when she turned to glare at him, he stood down.

She didn't say anything else, not until Bram had stopped fighting and brought it down to murmuring in his sleep. Finally, she turned to Sweet. "He's not an addict. He's dependent because he was on these meds at the hospital. He's having DTs because he didn't follow the correct protocol for weaning from powerful painkillers. It would've happened to anyone in his position. He just checked himself out of there too quickly . . ."

And got on the road to find his brother. "Can you really help him get better in three days?"

"If you cooperate."

"Me?"

"You can't always bend people to your will, Sweet," she reminded him.

"Misha, you have no idea—"

"I know you've got feelings for him and it's scaring the fuck out of you," Misha told him calmly. "Because I've never seen you do this to a civilian."

"He's a vet," Sweet said and Misha stared at him like his argument was the weakest shit ever.

"He's more than that to you."

"He betrayed Havoc."

"Really?" She looked around. "The club appears to be standing. Everyone in one piece except for Bram. And Linc. Any idea where Linc is?"

"Whose side are you on?"

"My patient's."

"He's my prisoner," Sweet reminder her.

Misha just gave him that small *I know more than you* smile she'd been giving him since childhood, and he gave up and walked out of the room.

He left the door open though. Just because Bram was unconscious at the moment didn't mean shit.

"You okay?" Gypsy asked. He was holding a container of food. "Fay sent this over for you. Said you need to eat."

Sweet didn't realize he was hungry until he smelled her signature meatloaf. He sat and began to eat as Gypsy stared into the room where Misha was helping Bram.

"Anything from him yet?" Gypsy asked finally.

"Not yet."

"He's fucked up."

"Tell me something I don't know."

Gypsy turned to Sweet and narrowed his eyes. "For all we know, he drugged himself."

"To what end?" Sweet sat back, half the dish gone, wishing Gypsy could give him a minute of motherfucking peace. Then again, Sweet had given all of Havoc a heart attack, so he owed them.

Gypsy shrugged. "Sympathy. To throw suspicion off him. Guilty conscience. Or maybe he was just trying to kill himself. Take your pick."

Sweet stared into the room where Misha was working on Bram. Boomer was helping her—he'd been a medic in the Marines, and he usually did a good triage until Misha arrived.

He didn't like pulling his sister into this shit, but she'd never had a problem proclaiming herself Havoc through and through. She also worked at a clinic downtown in her off hours from the hospital. This town knew and respected her. No one got turned away.

"You've got to deal with this now," Gypsy told him, his tone even despite the anger in his eyes.

"I know. But I'm not turning anyone over to Heathens."

"Even if he's one of them?"

"We'll take care of him on our own," Sweet reminded him.

"A lot of ways to take that."

"I mean if anything shakes out." Because if Bram was spying for Heathens, he'd have zero issue taking him out. No, he'd enjoy it for all the torture the Heathens had inflicted on Havoc and Shades Run over the years.

Sweet fisted his hands, hardened his heart, and prepared for the beginning of the end.

CHAPTER 18

STAY CLEAN

They must've called in Sweet's sister again—the doctor—because when Bram woke, he was in a bed and hazy in that happy, drug-fueled way that made him not give a shit how bad his life was at the moment.

He rolled over, wincing. He remembered slamming himself against the bars of the cell because he'd needed to get the fuck out of there.

"You okay?" Misha asked, handing him water and holding it for him so he didn't spill it. His hands were still shaking.

"The claustrophobia's new."

"Hell of a way to discover it."

"Tell me about it." Bram gingerly tested out sitting up and found himself less than successful at it. So he lay there on the pillow, trapped and sore. "The DTs . . ."

"Are better than they've been. You need time to get off all this shit."

"I don't have time."

"You seem to have plenty of it now," she told him, not unkindly.

He nodded. "Thanks for your help."

"Don't mention it. I'm not done yet. Anything else I can get you?"

He hadn't checked in with Dozer—and it was a necessity. "My phone—"

"Forget it," Sweet barked from the corner, and how the hell long had he been there?

Bram focused on him. "Gotta call Doz and check in before he calls in the cavalry. You can call him. But he'll want to hear from me."

Sweet narrowed his eyes. "Quick call. On speaker." He pulled Bram's phone out of his own pocket and flipped through the numbers.

He confirmed that he'd found the right one before he dialed and then he held it out toward Bram.

"Where the fuck have you been?" Dozer demanded.

"With Sweet—at Havoc. Detoxing."

Dozer blew out a hard breath. "You're all right then?"

"I'm alive and not with the Heathens. Best I can ask for right now."

"Right. Hey Sweet," Dozer called.

"Hey Dozer. Any surprises coming our way?" Sweet asked.

"I've managed to bury this, but Parisi's going to get suspicious soon—like when the Heathens' reports start coming in," Dozer admitted. "And Sweet? If you hurt him—"

"I know," Sweet said. "He's here. He's fine. He's not happy but he's fine. I'll have him call you again within twelve hours, but anything else comes up? You call me." Sweet rattled off a new number and Bram closed his eyes.

When Sweet ended the call, Bram opened them, and Sweet shook his head slowly and told him, "You need therapy."

"You provide that here under the Havoc protection plan?"

"Fuck you, Bram." Sweet pocketed Bram's phone.

"You need to call Heathens and demand to talk to Linc. If you won't, I will," Bram told him.

"Funny thing, you giving me orders."

"I'm not part of your MC."

"Bite the hand that feeds you a little more," Sweet warned.

"Why are you doing this, Sweet? I don't fucking get why you're putting all this at risk for me. You could've killed me. Handed me over. You probably should've done either of those things, but you brought me back here to what? Torture me? Save me? I can endure the first and I definitely don't need your help with the second." Bram pushed his luck, and no doubt Sweet's patience and all the biker's buttons.

Sweet yanked him up out of bed and slammed him against the wall. "You want to die, Bram. I get it. But you kill yourself on your own time."

"Let me go, Sweet." He heard the pleading in his voice and he hated it, hated that his words were both literal and not.

Sweet gave him the smallest of wry smiles. "I can't."

"You won't."

"Same thing."

"Why?"

"Same reason you kept me safe. Same reason you let me go."

With that, Bram's resistance left all at one, leaving him to lean his forehead against Sweet's. "It's all too much," he murmured.

"It seems that way. Break it down, it's not that bad."

"Right. Not until we get to the part about you telling Heathens I'm ATF."

"They won't find out from me," Sweet said tightly.

"You'll lie to your whole MC—"

"Never said that. I said Heathens won't find out. Havoc? They need to know."

Bram put his head back against the wall, his body suddenly too heavy again. Goddamned drugs. "I can't beg for acceptance. I won't."

"No one's asking you to."

"Yes, you are. You're asking me to prove myself. Again. And I'm tired of having to do that. I'm not fucking perfect but I've tried to make things better."

For Linc and Linnea. Mom. The town the Heathens lived in. Villages in the military. Himself even, at times.

And look where that's gotten you.

"Don't make a decision you'll regret," Sweet told him. "Because I've been there. Wish I could take it back. I'm trying to save you that trouble."

"What decision did you make that you regret?" Bram asked. Because if Sweet was going to ask him hard shit, he was going to force him to answer shit in kind.

Sweet stared at him, and when he spoke, there was an edge to his voice that shot up Bram's spine. "I killed the man I loved. That good enough for you?"

Yes, Bram supposed it was. "And you say I'm hard on myself. Takes one to know one, I guess."

"Don't push it."

"Fine. Let's go back to Linc. The Heathens have him."

Sweet narrowed his eyes. "You know that for sure?"

"Who the fuck else should we suspect? You didn't tell me anything about what Ozzie found out, but I'm not stupid."

"No, you're not," Sweet told him. "But you're the law, remember?"

"If you're not doing anything illegal, what's the problem?" Bram challenged.

"This isn't the time for your smart mouth."

Bram knew that, couldn't help himself. Whatever Sweet decided to do with him now, the one thing Bram could make sure of was that Sweet—or Havoc—didn't break him.

Never going to happen.

While Bram slept, Sweet made the call he'd been hesitant to. Bothering Ryker and Rush was risky. Putting anything personal into a man's head when he had a job to do could fuck him over. But Havoc might be in danger, so Sweet took the chance.

"Ryker, how's it going?" Sweet asked his trusted XO. Ryker had been away with Sean Rush, his partner and new recruit for Havoc, for the past several months working on a few things in the motor vehicle industry. Havoc loved its bikes but Rush loved his classic cars—faster the better—and using his expertise had so far proven invaluable.

It was through Ryker that Rush—and ultimately Linc—had come into their lives.

"We're good here. Job's looking to end a little later than we anticipated, but only because there's extra merchandise Sean's testing." Ryker sounded good—happy—and relaxed. Love would do that to a man.

"Good. Rush's okay, then?"

Ryker's voice immediately went to code red suspicious. "What's wrong?"

"I've got to talk to him about Linc. He's been missing for a month."

"No shit?"

"And his brother's here. But I want to talk to Rush cold about that—just tell him I need to talk to him about Linc's disappearance."

"You've got it. I'll put it on speaker. " There was a rustling and then, "Sweet, it's Rush. What's happening with Linc?"

"He's gone."

"Gone? Noah and I haven't heard shit from him, but I figured he was busy with Gypsy. Why the hell didn't you—"

"Hey Sweet," Ryker broke back in smoothly, stopping Rush's tirade. "That's not going to end well."

No, it wouldn't. And Rush was too new of a Havoc member to pull that shit. "Ask him about Linc's family and tell him to calm the fuck down or I'll pull him from the job," Sweet instructed. He heard some murmuring in the background and then Ryker said, "He's got an older sister and an older brother."

Sweet nodded, a sense of relief that his gut was still to be trusted. "Tell me about the brother."

But all Rush would say was, "Bram's a good guy," which led Sweet to believe that Rush knew what Bram did for a living.

"What's he do for a living?" Sweet pressed.

"He was in the military at one point . . . and then . . . you know," Rush hedged, then sighed. "I can't tell you what his job is now. Satisfied?"

"For now."

"Is Bram all right?" Rush asked Sweet. "Linc takes care of him, you know."

Sweet closed his eyes, the bond of the brothers weighing heavily on him. *Not your problem, or Havoc's.* But Rush was. Gypsy was.

Bram could bring the ATF, DEA, FBI all down on them, not to mention the local police and the DA. Rush could get arrested. Sweet wanted to believe that Bram wouldn't let that happen, but Bram couldn't be trusted. Linc could be working for him.

Then again, Bram hadn't given himself those scars. He hadn't drugged himself, and he'd tried to lead the Heathens away from Havoc.

Sweet had been the one bringing Bram, and the Heathens who followed, into Havoc. "Bram's in trouble, yes. Linc might be too."

"Because of Bram?" Rush asked tentatively.

"I know he's ATF," Sweet said quietly. Rush blew out a harsh breath, and Ryker cursed in the background. "Didn't you think it might be relevant to tell us?"

"No," Rush said firmly. "He's known me a long time. His jobs are big and complicated."

"How complicated?" Sweet demanded. "Because right now, I'm trying to decide if Bram walks away with his life."

"If he doesn't, Sweet . . ."

"You'll do what, Rush?"

Ryker knew better than to say a word.

"Leave Bram alone. He's a good guy. He takes down white supremacists who hurt women and children. He took down a chunk of the Heathens' meth business—tried to cripple it. It's about the meth part, not the MC part." Rush paused. "Linc's as much of a criminal as I am. Same with Bram—he just happened to channel it legally. I'm coming home and I'm going to find Linc. I'll take responsibility for Bram."

"Not your place," Sweet warned.

"Not yours either."

"Hang up now," Sweet told him and after a scuffle on the other end, with Ryker no doubt persuading him, Rush finally did just that.

Sweet went back into the room where Bram was. Misha was setting up another IV, but Bram was looking much better than he had a mere twenty-four hours earlier. Better than even an hour ago, which meant he was more dangerous. "Misha, I need a minute."

"No exertion," she warned.

"Misha," he growled and Bram snorted.

She wagged a finger at him and told Bram, "You heard me too. Stay in bed. Alone."

Bram smiled at her and waved, looking innocent as fuck. When Misha shut the door, the smile faded and he stared at Sweet like he was enemy number one.

"I made a call to Rush," Sweet told him. "He verified that you exist and that you are who you say you are."

"Wonderful. Always nice to have a car thief as my reference. So, am I allowed to live as per Havoc's good graces?" Bram asked, as unconcerned as he'd been earlier. An act—and a damned fine one at that—but an act nonetheless.

Sweet walked over to the bed even as Bram sat up as though ready for a fight. "You think Linc's been with the Heathens since your beatdown?"

"Maybe. Why though? Why not use him to get me back and let me know it? Send a message?" Bram shook his head. "Just let me hand myself to them if they have him. Trade me for Linc. Problem solved and I'll be out of your hair."

Jesus Christ. Bram said it like he was asking to go to the store for milk. The loyalty—the bond, the willingness to offer up his life for Linc's . . .

Sweet hadn't been wrong at all about him. Bram was exactly like a Havoc man. "We don't just hand over men to Heathens."

"You don't hand over your own," Bram corrected. "I'm not part of the Havoc family."

"Did you want to be?"

Bram shook his head tightly.

"Trying to be a goddamned hero."

"No," Bram said quietly. And that's when Sweet got it.

"You were trying to keep Havoc safe." And when Bram didn't answer, a muscle in his jaw jumped. "Bram, we protect ourselves."

"You shouldn't have to—at least not from my mistakes."

"It wasn't a mistake. You had a job. You should've been able to trust your boss."

Bram sagged a little, hanging his head. He was no doubt exhausted, more mentally than physically. Sweet sat next to him and caught him, pulled Bram against him until Bram put his head against his chest. "You're safe," Sweet told him. "You don't leave us behind. We won't desert you."

"I want to believe that."

"Then believe it."

"You don't have to protect me."

"I consider it protecting our investment."

"Right. Always comes back to business."

Sweet leaned in close. "Not always, love," Sweet murmured in his ear and felt Bram shudder with his next words. "Gonna end your pity party fast and hard, and then we'll set to figuring out what to do next."

CHAPTER 19

DROWN IF YOU WANT AND
I'LL SEE YOU AT THE BOTTOM

After another half a day on Misha-approved IVs, Bram was feeling better than he'd felt in a while. She'd given him pain pills that had far less of a narcotic effect than he'd been taking and instructed him to take ibuprofen and Tylenol round the clock in order to avoid the major aches and pains that led him into taking the pain pills in the first place.

"Most of all, take it easy," Misha told him sternly. "You need to rest."

Bram nodded, wanted to tell her that wasn't really up to him but Sweet broke in. "We've got this. I'll make sure he's okay."

"I'll be by later to check," Misha told him sweetly. "Where will I find him?"

Sweet didn't hesitate. "My place."

Bram frowned and Misha quirked her lip at her brother but didn't say anything to him. To Bram, she said, "Remember what I said. And here's a card with my number. Feel free to call me if you're feeling too much pain." She stuck the card into his hand and then she left without looking back at either of them.

Bram looked at Sweet, half expecting him to take the card, but Sweet just motioned for Bram to follow him. Bram tucked the card into his pocket and went with Sweet into his truck and stared out at the winding roads until they pulled in front of Sweet's house. Sweet got out of the truck without saying anything and Bram, after a moment of hesitation, did the same, walking into the house with more than a slight feeling of dread.

"I've got church in a few minutes. I need you to stay put, all right?"

"Got it," Bram muttered. "I'm sure most MC members want me still locked up."

"Probably."

"If they touch me, I'll fuck them all up. I'm not joking, Sweet."

He wasn't, because Sweet knew Bram could take on a hell of a lot of guys and, more than likely, come out the victor. Cuffs wouldn't hold him. Not for long. This sitting here almost free? This was a lot fucking harder.

He and Linc weren't brothers for nothing.

"Christ, you're an angry motherfucker."

"And you like it." Bram's eyes shot fire. He noted that Sweet didn't deny it. Couldn't. But Sweet did shake his head, like he'd known this was coming.

Hell, Bram had known it too, had ever since Sweet used the demonstrative *love* and then jacked him off.

"I can take your anger," Sweet told him, right before he walked out the door. "Just don't expect me to match it. I don't make decisions anymore when I'm angry. I did it once, and I'll regret it for the rest of my life."

Sweet couldn't deny it that he liked Bram's anger. Bram's fight. Because he'd denied himself for so long, to lead the MC with zero distraction post Jimmy-Boy.

Jimmy-Boy had been the biggest distraction of all, and at the time, Sweet thought he'd had it all under control. And maybe nobody noticed how out of control he'd been except Sweet himself.

And now, he was threatening to end up in the same situation. Using *love* as a demonstrative had been natural. Sincere.

And tonight Sweet had . . . watched Bram close off right before his eyes, which wasn't unexpected. But he knew Bram would stay. There was no way he'd risk Linc's life, and right now, Bram's own conscience was stronger than any chains. The only reason he'd risked Sweet's was because Sweet had backed him into a corner.

Bram had that same wary, cornered look in his eyes tonight. It was like dealing with a wild animal. Thankfully, Sweet had a lot of practice in talking down men like Bram . . . and thanks to several nights spent making Bram come, he had enough insight into the ATF agent to break him down . . . and maybe build him right back up.

Predictably, Bram couldn't sleep. Truthfully he didn't really try—mainly paced the house like an angry lion before finally going out onto the deck off Sweet's bedroom and sitting under the moonlight with a bottle of scotch he'd snagged earlier from downstairs.

But just the smell made him feel sick. He'd told Misha that he wouldn't drink for a while, until he got on his feet and made sure he was over self-medicating. And he felt guilty for fucking with her trust.

So instead, he put the bottle down and stood, looked over the rails toward the roads that led to the middle of the property. He could jump down and follow it along but he couldn't get far. If he couldn't have one type of escape . . .

"You really want to go?" Sweet asked from behind.

Ah fuck. "Why don't you just tell me what I can and can't do, Daddy."

Sweet was on him in a second. "You lookin' for a daddy? Because I wouldn't mind spending time teaching you a few things."

Then Sweet walked away. And that made Bram's angry motherfucker come right back out to play. Again.

He ran, light and quiet, and slammed Sweet from behind. Sweet clearly hadn't expected him to have the balls—or the stupidity—to do that. Bram knocked him flat, held him down, whispered in his ear, "Just because it's your place doesn't mean you get to call my shots."

"You don't get the whole authority thing, do you?"

"Get it. Hate it. Don't plan on following it," Bram growled.

Sweet tensed up, readying himself for a fight. They were evenly matched, and even hurt and detoxing, Bram was a strong fucker.

But just as suddenly as Bram knocked him down, he got up. Sweet followed, getting onto his feet and facing Bram, standing inches from him. And that's when Bram surprised Sweet in a way he never thought he could be surprised again.

Bram faced him. And then he dropped, purposefully, to his knees directly in front of Sweet. Put his head forward to rest on Sweet's thigh.

But Sweet didn't mistake this for Bram giving up or giving in.

"Christ, Bram, just when I think . . ." He trailed off as he brushed his knuckles along Bram's cheekbone. "So fucking full of surprises. You're killing me."

Bram looked down pointedly at Sweet's obviously hard cock. "I can help fix that. I can try to help fix everything, Sweet, but you have to let me. You can't—" His voice broke.

"You've got to let me lead, Bram. And you've got to trust me."

"Wouldn't be down here if I didn't."

"We'll figure it out, baby. If that's what you want."

"I want you. I want Linc safe. Beyond that . . ."

"That's a pretty damned good start." Somehow, he'd been dancing around Bram like he was Jimmy's ghost. This? Solidified that Bram was nothing of the goddamned sort.

Bram was needy for this, but the guy was also an island. He could live alone for a long time and make it, but he'd thrive in a place like Havoc.

Bram needed healing, but he would heal. The hurt-comfort cycle wasn't what he needed. He needed the rough stretch of sex . . . but he could also provide enough comfort for himself and a partner.

"You don't know what I had to sit back and watch," Bram bit out.

"Did the good you did outweigh the bad you needed to let happen?"

"I can't do that, Sweet. Can't play judge and jury, balancing the scales."

Sweet stroked his hair. "You have to, Bram. Otherwise, you won't make it."

"Then maybe I won't make it," Bram admitted, maybe out loud for the first time.

"You're a good man."

"No, that's not true. I was. A good man doesn't stand by and watch people getting killed."

"Pretty sure Heathens kill a lot of scum too, including each other. Also pretty sure what you did helped to save a lot of people from them in the future, right?"

"Stop trying to make me feel better."

"You're still in fucking shock. PTSD," Sweet told him. "You've got to trust me more than you trust yourself."

Bram stared at him. "I can promise you that for tonight. That's all I have right now."

"It's enough."

Sweet tugged Bram to his feet, held him close. "I want to know every goddamned thing that turns you on. Every forbidden desire. Every desire that scares the fuck out of you, and I want to show you ones you didn't even know you had."

Bram put his forehead down on Sweet's shoulder as he surrendered. Again. There were a myriad of other choices he could make but none of them felt this right.

He let himself be led into Sweet's room, let himself be stripped and told to, "Get on the bed—on your back," in Sweet's darkest, hottest drawl.

Bram's skin prickled, from cold and a little fear and anticipation. Sweet took out a piece of rope. "Arms up—over your head."

Bram did as he asked, wrapping his fingers around the lowest rung of the headboard as Sweet tied his wrists together with the rope that was softer than he'd expected. Sweet tied him well, not too tight, and Bram was reasonably sure he could get out of it . . . eventually. But with Sweet's heavy body on his?

No.

Sweet remained clothed as he knelt between Bram's legs, spreading them wide, one hand stroking his cock and the other drifting along his chest and sides, over the scars, new and old, touching them with rough fingertips before finally pressing a finger between his legs, fingering him, demanding Bram to simply take it.

The restraints made him raw. Helpless. Exposed. He shuddered when Sweet's finger breeched his hole, dry.

"That's right. You're going to let me do what I need to. Just shut up and for fucking once, we're going to shut off that goddamned mind of yours."

A groan escaped from Bram's mouth as Sweet's finger pushed in and took him—not painful, just different with no lube.

But when he touched Bram's gland over and over, Bram gripped the headboard bar tightly to not crumble. Sweet smiled and took his hand off Bram's cock and reached for something on the bed next to him.

He held them up for a second, and Bram recognized them immediately, opening his mouth to say *no* when Sweet said, "Your safeword?"

Bram closed his eyes, feeling Sweet's finger still inside of him. "Fed."

The word was part challenge, a last-minute way to make Sweet realize what he was doing and who Bram really was.

Sweet stroked his shoulder, and then Bram felt the bite of the clamps on his nipples, one after the other, pulling a wicked burn of pleasure from him. Bram's chest surged up to meet the bites of pain. "Fuck. Fuck!"

"Yeah, that'll happen," Sweet assured him. His finger left Bram for a minute, and then two lubed fingers disappeared inside of him.

"Stop thinking. Just fucking feel," Sweet growled as he added another finger, and yes, Bram did, his balls tightening, his cock stretched tight and ready to come.

"Such a pretty cock. Thinking of piercing it," Sweet said seriously. Bram gasped, a half sob as Sweet twisted his fingers—four of them now—inside him. "And I could do that. Call the piercers in here right now. And what could you do?"

"Nothing," Bram gasped.

"He'd come in here, see you splayed out, needy as fuck, my hand in your ass and he'd stand here and play with your cock, looking for just the right place." As Bram nodded, Sweet reached up to his clamped nipples. "Or maybe I should do these instead."

He took a clamp off suddenly, with no warning.

"Fuck," Bram shouted, the blood rushing as the metal came off and his ass clamped hard around Sweet's fingers, trapping them there as he shot come up his chest.

"Didn't have permission to do that," Sweet said as Bram came back down to earth, still spread on Sweet's fingers. He was drunk on Sweet, a desire that was hot and needy unfurling so damned slowly as he realized that Sweet had started sliding his hand inside farther. That Sweet's thumb had joined his fingers, and they were working him, slowly. Purposefully.

Sweet nodded, watching him carefully, stroking and kneading his cock with his free hand. "Yes, baby. All five in there. Stay still."

"No. Nononono," Bram moaned, but in reality, he'd fucking die if Sweet stopped now. Because it seemed like Sweet had been playing with him for a minute, for an hour . . . he'd lost track of time, aware only of his skin, slick with sweat, his moans of satisfaction, the way his ass took Sweet in . . .

The way he was holding himself still so Sweet could take him exactly the way he wanted to. The way both of them wanted. It was predatory. Dirty.

Perfect.

"Look down," Sweet commanded.

Bram didn't want to, but he didn't want to disobey Sweet. He saw Sweet's wrist at the same time he felt Sweet's hand attempt to open inside his ass. A dark thread of satisfaction unraveled, deep in his belly. His climax exploded and everything went white and floaty, and he went to that special place Sweet seemed to bring him to easily. A place where nothing mattered except Sweet. And pleasure.

Then he was shuddering. Moaning, cursing.

He was so empty, but almost instantly Sweet's cock filled him, and his ass clamped down, adjusted, and Sweet gave him the ride of his life.

Bram could barely hang on—and he did hang on as Sweet pounded him. They were loud. Anyone walking by—hell, anyone in the general vicinity—knew what they were doing.

"Yell, baby. Yell my name. Let them all know you're claimed."

He did. It was all *Sweet* and *yes* and *please* and *yours.* Anything Sweet told him. Nothing to do with getting out of trouble and more about wanting Sweet to keep him. In his bed.

In his life.

Bram was knocked out, sleeping peacefully for probably the first time in God knew how long. And while he slept, Sweet planned. Because the danger—to Bram, to Havoc, was far from over. No, the doors had opened up to let in a world of problems.

CHAPTER 20

GO ON AND SAVE YOURSELF

Bram woke from the nightmare with a yell and Sweet's voice trying to calm him down. Bram sat up, panting, sweating, trying to get his mind around where the fuck he was.

"Bram, you're with me. At Havoc. Safe," Sweet told him, and Bram snorted.

"Right. Safe." He tried to push away but Sweet held him there.

"What the fuck happened to you, Bram? I know your sup screwed you good but . . . this was something else."

"It's nothing," he mumbled.

"It's not nothing—and it keeps coming up to bite you in the ass."

"Linc's father tried to fucking kill us," he blurted out without warning, and Sweet did let him up then. Bram paced a little while he talked. "My own dad sucked but my stepdad? If he wasn't ordering us around drunk he was hitting me. The day he tried to kill me and Linc was the day I realized I could never fucking fully trust anyone, especially not someone in a position of authority. Are you satisfied now?"

Sweet sighed. "I'm sorry your stepfather was fucked up."

"I don't need your sympathy," Bram spat, his skin hot and tingly.

"Sweet, we both know this can't go anywhere."

"Who says?"

It was Bram's turn to sigh. "Even if I wasn't who I am, you think the club's going to accept you with an outsider?"

"They did before," Sweet said.

"This is crazy," Bram muttered. "Fucking nuts."

"Maybe you need to shut up and go with it," Sweet suggested.

"Maybe I've done that too many times in my life."

"Bram," Sweet said quietly. "What we did tonight . . . it was intense. This reaction? It's normal."

"Thanks for the analysis. Know I can always count on you for it." As his head cleared, he decided that maybe it was time to turn the tables on Sweet a little, put his feet to the fire, as it were, and get some answers he probably didn't deserve. "You and Jimmy played." It was a statement, not a question.

"He needed it," was all Sweet said, his voice as tight as his expression. He was done with this conversation. Bram?

Wasn't. "Did you?"

"Did I what?"

"Need it?"

Sweet swallowed. "I needed him."

Jesus, Sweet's loss was palpable. "Do you still play?"

"Why aren't you letting this go?"

"Because you've played with me," Bram told him, and Sweet's head snapped up. Then he walked toward Bram with a dangerous stride. "Are you denying it?"

"Why are you pressing?"

Because I won't let you dismiss what you've done with me. "Because most people who enjoy this kind of play don't just do it because one person enjoys it. That never works, and you and Jimmy? Sounds like you worked."

"You don't get to analyze my sex life, or any part of my personal life. Hell, any part of my life."

And right there, Bram had his answer, the one he'd been pushing for. The one he'd already known despite the fact that a small part of him still hoped it would be different. "Got it. Subject dropped."

It wasn't, though, if Bram's expression was any indication. He'd shuttered off again, and although he'd pissed Sweet off, Sweet couldn't deny Bram had been right. Like Bram, Sweet liked the fight—and he liked to win. Not letting Bram analyze him was hypocritical as hell, but Sweet hadn't been pushed by anyone on this since Jimmy-Boy. It wasn't a place Sweet willingly liked to go back to.

Because Jimmy-Boy hadn't so much needed him as he'd needed someone to constantly be there to save him. He wanted a full-time Dom . . . and Sweet had tried to be one. Tried his best to constantly give Jimmy what he needed. But it became apparent that Jimmy didn't even know what he truly wanted or needed—and he refused to try to figure it out. And he definitely didn't want to let Sweet know any of his needs, contented himself by telling Sweet that he wasn't helping. Forcing Sweet to try to push his limits. But what Jimmy needed was beyond simply wanting to be a sub.

He went back into the military after they broke up and told Sweet that he'd be sorry. Sweet had hated that they'd left it like that . . . and even though he knew he had nothing to do with the fact that Jimmy was killed in combat, the guilt still hung heavily. After Jimmy-Boy, he'd stuck to threesomes. Easier, with no entanglements. That was why he'd been happy when Grayson jumped into his first night with Bram.

But when Sweet hadn't considered bringing in a third after that, he knew he was in trouble. Then, and now. He admitted the partial truth, knowing it would piss Bram off. "Jimmy-Boy wanted to be saved. He was as addicted to it as I was to saving him."

Bram just looked at him, more upset than angry, but obviously comparing their situation to the one Sweet just described. "I guess you think you've got a type then."

"Bram . . ."

"You think I've enjoyed being saved by you? You think I like being fucking helpless? Because I hate it. I've worked to get us to an even ground. I'm not looking to be dominated, Sweet. I like playing with you, and that's obvious, but I'm not looking to be saved."

"I know that."

"No. I don't think you do." Bram pointed at him. "It's one thing to know I'll be compared by everyone in this club and you to the ghost of a guy who fucked you up badly. But now you're telling me he was fucked up the entire time you were together, and that's supposed to make me feel better how?" Bram shook his head. "I've survived for a hell of a long time on my own. I've kept a lot of people safe, including myself. I might love the danger of my job, of rough sex, but I'm not unstable enough to go looking for danger just because. Anything I've done? Has been to save Linc. And you. Tell me, Sweet, did Jimmy-Boy ever do anything to save you . . . or is that all you need from a guy? If it is, then ain't ever gonna work."

Sweet knew Bram was freaked out—and lashing out. Hell, he was too. He couldn't deny that. They'd both been through hell, and neither one of them seemed ready to climb on out completely. And before he could stop himself, Sweet was reminding him, "You're the one who said this can't go anywhere. Stop trying to blame it on me."

"You're keeping me on the outside. Do you not see that? I can't ask a question about the last serious relationship you've had, but you want total honesty from me?"

Sweet tried to keep his patience, but Bram was purposely pushing buttons and sometimes you got what you asked for. "You've said repeatedly that you don't want to be here. You've said you're only here for Linc, that you just wanted to pay and get the fuck out of here. You lied to all of us. And then you're pissed that you're treated like an outsider. Bram, you are."

"I know." He said it angrily. "You want me to wear it painted on my forehead? I guess I don't have to—everyone fucking knows I don't belong."

Being a loner had never bothered Bram until he realized that having no one to count on at the end of the day, no one to go home to and find comfort with really fucking sucked.

"Bram, look—"

"Don't, Sweet, okay? Don't try to make it better."

"Who the fuck you think you're talking to?" Sweet demanded.

"The only reason I'm still alive, right? That's your big threat. You know what? I'm not hanging around because of a threat, Sweet. Newsflash—I'm hanging out because I want to hang out with you. You think I couldn't leave if I wanted to? You think I couldn't escape? Trust me, I've gotten out of worse scrapes in my life."

Sweet looked at him oddly and Bram's inner alarms were going off, clanging loudly and telling him to shut the fuck up.

Bram, of course, ignored that, because why use common sense in a situation like this? Where the fuck had common sense gotten him until now? Almost killed. "So how about I just go, all right?"

"Is that what you want?"

No, it wasn't. But he'd be damned if he admitted what he wanted now.

"God, you're fucked up, Bram." Sweet's words were gentle. "You've been to hell and back. I realize that. That's why I brought you here."

"To make me feel worse?"

"I realize it seems like that, but no, my intent was to help."

"I'm not a charity case."

"You wouldn't be here if you were," Sweet agreed. "Jimmy was my everything. He wasn't a Havoc member but he was active-duty military. Maybe when he got out he would've become Havoc or maybe he just would've stayed the way he was. It wouldn't have mattered to me."

"How long?" Bram managed.

"Five years. I was twenty-four and he was twenty-one when we first met." Sweet glanced over at Jimmy's picture. "We got into a fight before he shipped out for the last time. We actually broke up. Or at least, I broke up with him. I told him I wanted him out, and he signed up for six more years. He told me . . ." Sweet wore a pained expression. "That just because I was going to run Havoc didn't mean I could run him and his life. So I told him that I couldn't keep watching him go into battle and come back with all the scars, physical and mental. I told him I couldn't and that if he walked out the door to never come back." Sweet looked at the ceiling and laughed. "The fucker never did. Got KIA two months in. And even though he wrote and called, I fucking ignored him. I might as well have put the bullet—"

"Stop," Bram told him firmly. "He didn't believe that. You can't either. Stop fucking punishing yourself for something that wasn't your fault. You're guilty of wanting someone you loved to be safe. That's it."

Sweet stared at him. "I want to believe that."

"Then do it. Set yourself free. You don't deserve it. And although I don't know Jimmy, I've got to believe he would be pissed at you for blaming yourself."

"Yeah, he would. He'd call me a control freak."

Bram shrugged. "If the shoe fits."

Sweet's eyes narrowed. "Funny, but you don't seem to mind it when you're coming."

"Never said I minded it at all. From certain people." Bram paused. "I'm really sorry about Jimmy. He sounds like a good guy."

Sweet nodded. "I don't want to talk about him anymore."

"Right. Got it." Bram closed off again.

"Why do you do that?" Sweet demanded.

"What?"

"You shutter yourself up, like you're keeping the world out. Keeping me out."

"Because I don't need to keep banging my head against a wall. Okay? I get it. You don't want to talk about Jimmy with me. There'll never be anyone like him for you again."

"Bram—"

"Don't, okay? I'm just stating facts. I've been on my own for a long time. Long enough to know that I can pop in and out of places but not find a home there. I got that early on. I don't expect anything. But dammit, don't try to kid me into believing anything."

Sweet stood with him. Bram felt like a fucking fool and tried to push him away, but Sweet wouldn't let go of him.

"Sweet, I'm going to push you off me any way I can. Don't corner me. Don't."

Sweet let him go, stood back with his hands up. "I'm not trying to fool you or lead you on."

"But?"

"Don't you realize why this has been so hard for me? If I didn't have feelings for you, the first ones I've had for anyone since Jimmy died, I wouldn't be this fucked up."

Bram's breath caught. "I didn't come here for this."

"I didn't bring you here for this. Not at first."

"Great. So neither of us wanted this. I'll fucking pay you for Linc and go find him. You don't have to do anything else for me. You're digging yourself and your club deeper and deeper."

"And I don't give a shit if it means not losing you. So how fucked do you think that makes me?" Sweet asked him in a low and dangerous voice. "You planning on screwing me?"

"I've never done that. I have no plans to do it in the future."

"Anything else you're not telling me?"

Bram gave a dull laugh as exhaustion hit him hard again. He lay back against the pillow and stared at the ceiling. "I've told you more than I've ever told anyone in my fucking life. What more do you want from me?"

Sweet stared at him but didn't answer. And even though he didn't want to admit it, that scared Bram a little more than anything else at the moment.

CHAPTER 21

KICKED IN THE TEETH

It was time to check in with Dozer again. Bram called him, the phone on speaker so Sweet could listen in on the conversation.

"How're you feeling?" Dozer asked.

Bram slid a glance over to Sweet. "Better now. Anything on Linc?"

"Nothing. Sorry, man. It's been quiet on Parisi's end. I've been through all his files and his texts—no mention of your brother. Nothing in your files either."

Bram rubbed a hand along the back of his neck. Dozer was good enough not to get caught and besides that, the heat must be on Parisi at this point. If he couldn't turn Bram into the Heathens, Parisi could be screwed from both ends. "There's still the matter of the drugging. Gypsy's credit check might've let Parisi know I was in town. From there, he obviously tied me to Havoc."

"So who drugged you? Would someone from Havoc have been turned?" Dozer asked.

"By Heathens? No. By the law? Definitely not."

"Unless Parisi was holding something over them," Dozer said. "Or else there are non-Havoc people on the compound."

For the party, there might've been. Also, there were other operations happening and all the people involved weren't MC members. He'd been paranoid about bikers. Would he have noticed a really good tail from another agent? He went from freezing cold to angry as fire. "I'm taking Parisi down."

"Easy, tiger. Right now, it's open season and you're top billing on the kill list."

Right. Hidden at Havoc. Sold out. "You think the tail's here?"

"Maybe they're undercover on the compound. Like you."

Bram fought the urge to correct Dozer, because technically, the man was correct. "Are there any new guys around, or is it just me?"

Sweet's eyes narrowed. "Wait here."

Oh shit. The look on Sweet's face was seriously scary and turned Bram the fuck on at the same time. To Dozer, he said, "I think Sweet's got someone in mind."

"Call me when you've got him and I'll run him. Meantime, you're safest at Havoc." Dozer paused, then laughed. "Said no one ever."

"Yeah," Bram sighed, signed off and stared after Sweet's retreating back.

"What's up?" Tug asked as Sweet marched into the clubhouse with a purpose.

"I need to check out the new people on board for the films."

Films meant the porn that got shot on Havoc land. The actors were heavily supervised and bodyguarded and off-limits, the sets restricted to necessary crew only. It was all on the up-and-up, willing and consensual, *and* made Havoc a fuck-load of money. It also kept the feds away. Havoc paid their share of taxes.

More than.

"Anyone in particular?" Tug asked.

"Newest hires. Maybe not actors," Sweet told him. Together, they walked into the main office, where one of the brothers who managed the books for the place sat, watching the monitor.

"Working hard, JohnO?" Sweet asked.

"Perks of the job." JohnO glanced over at Sweet. "How can I help, brother?"

"Need a list of new hires. Pictures too."

"You got it." JohnO went into a file cabinet that looked like hell on wheels and pulled the records out immediately. "We only hired two new ones in the past couple of months. Everyone else has been here at least a year or more. Both these guys were vetted thoroughly."

Sweet paged through quickly, pulled out forms on the two men and stared at the pictures. One of them boasted a military background. He held the paper out to Tug. "Bring him to me."

"Any place in particular?"

"Basement of the clubhouse. Don't get him comfortable," Sweet ordered.

"Works for me," Tug said. "JohnO, looks like you'll be needing a new hire."

"Tell me about it. Sorry, boss. Thought he seemed like he'd work out. I like to give vets a hand."

Sweet nodded. "I get it. This one's a special case—don't let it stop you from doing it again."

With the man JohnO flagged secured in the cell in the basement of the clubhouse, Sweet pulled in Gypsy, Tug, and Ozzie.

Sweet got Gypsy and Ozzie up-to-date about the traitor.

"You think he's the one who drugged Bram?" Ozzie asked. "Because if that's true, he's been in contact with the ATF."

"Or the Heathens," Tug said. "I'm not sure which is fucking worse at this point."

"Bram is worse," Gypsy muttered.

Sweet stiffened but kept his cool, reminding them all, "Bram was betrayed."

"He was betraying another MC." Tug crossed his arms for emphasis, mind made up.

Ozzie shrugged unapologetically. "Heathens though."

"Still an MC," Tug insisted.

Sweet knew they could go on all day. "We hate them and everything they represent. Bram was attempting to stop their meth trade. Plus, they treat their women like shit," he reasoned. Gypsy remained silent, Tug crossed his arms, and Ozzie nodded at Sweet. "Bram wasn't trying to shut them down because they were one-percenters. Plus, it was his job. He didn't randomly go there. It's not like he's trying to hurt our MC."

"How do we know?" Gypsy finally demanded. "Right now, the game he's running has been pretty effective. Pretend your hiding from your other undercover job. In effect, he's been here undercover, right? How's that different? He's still with the ATF, am I right?"

"He's learned nothing that could compromise us," Sweet said.

"I know that you believe that, Sweet. I really do," Gypsy said. "But we've got to be fuckin' careful."

It took Bram all of three seconds to make the guy as an ATF asset, which was way different than an actual ATF agent. Parisi had threatened to expose the asset named Mike to the drug dealers he'd been working over for the ATF, forcing him to get a job on Havoc's porn set. It was a smart move, because the only non-Havoc members who worked there were the porn stars themselves. Bram couldn't decide if it was the best—or the shittiest—undercover job ever, but right about now he'd bet the guy would say the latter. Because he was tied up, and he'd been interrogated by Havoc before Bram had gotten to him.

Not that Bram would've been any kinder. The ATF's tenet on most low-level assets was, *"If you're caught and we don't know, you're completely on your own."*

Obviously, this asset hadn't gotten the memo, because he bit out, "You can't kill me," to Bram.

"Actually, I can. Because I know you as a porn star who tried to kill me. The agency's not going to give itself away for you. They'll let you take the blame, no harm, no foul."

Mike went pale. "I didn't have any choice."

Bram knew all about following orders. He could even drum up some sympathy for the poor bastard.

"He said he was told to kill you and frame us or the Heathens," Tug confirmed, and he didn't seem happy about it. At least it wasn't Bram he was unhappy with this time.

"So what now?" Gypsy was asking Sweet when Bram walked out of the basement and into the office. It was the first time he and Gypsy had come face-to-face with one another while Bram was conscious since their fight. Since Bram admitted to being ATF. Gypsy narrowed his eyes and looked between the men, but continued to only address Sweet. "Because we can't keep anyone with ATF ties shackled in our basement forever."

Bram stared at Gypsy and said, "He's not an agent. He's an asset. Disposable. But I'd keep him in play for a little longer."

"If by 'in play' you mean in that cell, I'm fine with that," Sweet told him. "Parisi is the far bigger problem."

"But the question is why?" Gypsy asked. "Why go to the trouble of planting Bram as undercover and letting him figuratively deflate the shit out of the Heathens . . . only to turn him in? The ATF got what they wanted."

"Maybe Bram did too good a job," Sweet said slowly, pinning his full attention to Bram. "Maybe your sup sent you in to get evidence. Then Parisi goes to the Heathens and says, 'I'll bury your MC unless you cut me in on the deal.'"

"And the only way that would work is if their witness—me— ended up dead," Bram said slowly.

"Not necessarily. You could get out clean and never be the wiser . . . so why would Parisi sell you out?"

Bram swallowed hard before admitting, "I've got a bank account number—and the records that tie it to Parisi, although I didn't know it at the time. It's for my own protection. When I told Parisi about it . . . that was the night before I was attacked. I told him I thought the account number would be enough to get the heroin dealer, that I wouldn't have to patch in. So I'm supposed to come back from my vacation and do my final report. Then the heat will go back on the Heathens so they can't connect the two timelines."

"Looks like Parisi wants to ensure that you didn't make it that far."

"What if the evidence you have ties Parisi in?" Sweet asked. "What if he's covering enough for the Heathens? Enough to make money. He can't stop the investigation completely, but he says 'I'll look into it. I have resources. I'll find your missing member.' They don't have to know he's ATF."

Gypsy nodded slowly. "Parisi is the enemy. Right now, they think Bram's a probie with too much information. Imagine what would happen if they knew the truth about who he really was? And I'm not seeing a way around that if it's between Parisi getting himself fucked or Bram getting dead."

Bram winced, but Gypsy was only laying out the truth, and it was one Bram already knew.

"I need to see Jethro," Bram told them.

"You know Jethro?" Sweet asked carefully.

"Yeah, I know Jethro."

"I didn't think he hung around with Heathens," Gypsy pointed out.

"How well do you know him?" Sweet pressed Bram.

"How well do you know him?" Bram shot back.

Sweet growled at the game of chicken happening. "I'll talk to Jethro. You're staying here."

"You should've let me kill him when I had the chance," Gypsy said.

"Which one?" Sweet asked.

"Both of them."

CHAPTER 22

YOUR TIME IS GONNA COME

Sweet sent Bram over to the diner. Bram left easily, like he didn't want to be involved in anything that might happen to the asset.

But Tug had things on his mind. "Okay, Sweet, you're proving your point about Bram. He was set up. I heard it firsthand from Mike. But what now? Are we covering for Bram with the Heathens? Because I say yes."

"I second that," Ozzie said.

Sweet turned his attention to Gypsy to see what he thought about it.

"We could tell the Heathens that we know Bram was their probie but that we patched him into Havoc," Gypsy reasoned. "Because technically, there's nothing on the bylaws about patching in another club's probie."

Sweet played devil's advocate. "And if Bram's supervisor decides to spill what Bram's real job is?"

"We say we didn't know. We send him away and tell Heathens we killed him," Gypsy said.

It wasn't a bad plan, but Sweet didn't like loose ends. Parisi was one of them. "It's time to call Jethro."

Jethro was an undercover ATF agent with the Hangmen MC. Casey, the club's president, knew who and what Jethro was. Sweet didn't ask too much more about it, but he figured that it had to be a mutually beneficial relationship for both the MC and the ATF. Which was odd, considering the Hangmen stole high-end cars, like Havoc.

The one thing the clubs did have in common was the zero tolerance for drugs policy—selling for sure was a major no, and taking? No hard drugs, recreational only—and mainly pot. Both MCs had too much to lose to get caught up in the drug race.

Sweet figured Jethro helped keep the Colombians off the Hangmen's backs—oftentimes, MCs were pressured into helping drug lords with their businesses in return for money . . . and protection.

That's not why the Heathens sold meth, though.

Two hours after they left Havoc, Bram was in Ozzie's care at Havoc and Sweet was at the Hangmen's compound with Tug, telling Jethro, "I need a lead on a guy named Parisi."

Jethro leaned back, a booted foot on the desk. "I'm not for fucking hire, Sweet."

Casey stared between the two of them. "Sweet, I owe you, man, and you owe me. This one? Between you two."

Sweet nodded and Casey left him and Jethro alone. "It's for Linc's brother. Bram."

If Jethro knew who Bram was or what he'd been doing, he didn't give anything away. "Again, I'm not in the habit of selling out my brothers. Just like you."

Sweet passed him Dozer's number. "Call him. I told him you'd be asking him questions. See for yourself how good a brother Parisi is. Maybe there's a medal in it for you."

Jethro snorted but he took the number.

"He's a strong motherfucker. A group of Heathens beat the shit out of him. He's like fucking bionic or something. I won't fuck with him."

"Sweet doesn't seem to mind. Then again, he hasn't been with anyone like this since Jimmy-Boy.

"Hope this guy doesn't screw with him."

"Any more than he already has."

"You don't trust Sweet's judgment?"

"Always. But that doesn't mean I can't watch his back at the same time."

The Havoc members were glancing over to where Bram was punching the bag, talking freely since he appeared oblivious to their conversation.

In reality, he heard every goddamned word, which contributed to the ferocity of his workout. It had been months since he'd been able to stretch his muscles like this, and he worked through the pain and the burn, not caring how much he'd hurt afterwards.

It was either take it out on the bag or the men around him, and that wouldn't fly. Like Linc, he had impulse issues but he didn't have Linc's charm. He was more the brute force or the quiet one often underestimated.

Obviously, that wasn't happening here. His rep preceded him and that was a good thing, because he wasn't sure he was ready to handle another group beatdown. But after Sweet had walked out of his house, Bram couldn't stand staring at the walls wondering what the fuck had happened now. Ozzie hadn't given him any trouble about coming to the gym, but now, Bram was starting to wonder if he'd been set up.

"Need help?" One of the guys came over and held onto the bag so Bram could get some better hits off it.

"Yeah. Thanks." Bram continued hitting the bag as the guy said, "I'm Boomer."

"Bram."

"Yeah, know that. Wanna spar?"

Bram stopped and looked at him. The guy was around his age, in good shape. Was this a setup or a necessary evil of being here with Sweet? But he was already taped up so he said, "Sure," and headed toward the ring in the middle of the gym.

It was midday but still pretty crowded in here. Of course, guys stopped what they were doing when he and Boomer started throwing hits.

Bram got into a rhythm quickly. Boomer was a good partner for this, and obviously talented. Although Bram could take the guy in hand-to-hand, boxing required a subtlety that not many MMA and street fighters could master and Boomer gave him a mix of both. "You're pro?" Bram asked as he ducked from Boomer's left.

"Trying to distract me with compliments?"

"No, but thanks for the idea."

Boomer swore as Bram blocked a sharp left hook and gave Boomer a good blow to the stomach and then hooked a leg around Boomer's calf to take him down to the mat. "Fucker."

"Thanks," Bram said with a smile.

"Anytime," Boomer groaned. "Sweet's got my number if you want to do it again."

Bram wondered what the protocol was for that, if Boomer couldn't just call Bram directly because he was "with" Sweet. If Bram was a chick, then yeah, that shit wouldn't fly, but did the same rules apply to anyone the men were dating?

And that was something he never thought he'd worry about—rules of dating someone in an MC. Christ, what the hell was happening to his life?

By the time he went back to Sweet's to shower, Sweet was there, waiting for him. "Heard you put on a show."

"I would've had it taped if I thought you'd be this interested."

"Watching you fight? Yeah, I'm interested."

"Even though it's not with you?"

Sweet shrugged. "Still a turn-on."

"Boomer's not allowed to call me directly, I guess."

Sweet threw his head back and laughed. "Hey, at least they're not discriminating."

"Yeah, well, I'm not exactly your old lady on display." As soon as the words came out of his mouth, Bram knew he'd left himself wide-open.

Sweet came up behind him. "Is that what you want? Planning on letting me put you on display for the club?"

Jesus. Bram shuddered at the thought. Not the actual doing, though, because no. But as a fantasy . . .

"Yeah, baby likes that. Maybe I'll lay you out in the ring, naked. Or take you in the showers there with everyone watching. You like to be cheered on?" Sweet nipped the skin on his shoulder, hard enough to make Bram even harder than he already was, at the same time his hand wrapped around Bram's cock.

"Fuck, Sweet . . ."

Sweet chuckled and dragged him into the shower.

Afterward, they got into bed and lay under the ceiling fan, until Bram started to shiver. Sweet grabbed him a blanket and they remained there, watching the sun set in comfortable silence.

"I'm guessing no leads on Linc yet," Bram asked. For the thousandth time since Sweet put out feelers.

"Hasn't even been a full twenty-four hours," Sweet reminded him. His answer varied depending on how much time had passed since Bram last asked.

"I never said patience was my strong suit."

"Who am I kidding—not mine either. But I fake it better than you." Sweet rolled onto his side. "You up for celebrating tonight?"

"Celebrating what?"

"How about just being alive?"

Bram shrugged. "Since I am, doesn't seem like a bad reason at all."

CHAPTER 23

GOT YOU BY THE BALLS

Sweet never heard back from Jethro. Not directly. But sometime in the predawn hours, Tug called him to say that there'd been a bag delivered—with a man inside, bound and gagged—at the end of the property.

Sweet had no doubt who the present was.

Parisi.

So Sweet went to the clubhouse to wait for their new prisoner to be transported up the hill, leaving Bram sleeping. Between the sex and the pain pill (Misha-approved), he was out, emotionally and physically. Sweet hated watching how it killed him not to ask about Linc every five minutes, but if Bram wasn't cleared, and soon, he wasn't going to do Linc much good at all. Wherever he was.

Tug and Ozzie must've alerted Gypsy too, because he was in the clubhouse ahead of Sweet. He anticipated a fight, a warning that holding an ATF agent was enough to take the entire Havoc MC down.

But nothing. Which meant that Gypsy believed Parisi was dirty.

"Are you going to tape a confession?" Gypsy asked.

"Smart thing to do, right?" Sweet said.

Gypsy shrugged. "If you were going to let him live, I guess. We can always destroy the tape."

Sweet nodded slowly and watched Tug and Ozzie carry the man wrapped in burlap in and down the stairs. Parisi was struggling a little but was tied too tightly to do much at all.

"Does Bram know he's here?" Gypsy asked.

"Not yet. Maybe never. Figured it was better to hear Parisi out first."

"And if you find out Bram's lying?"

"Then we turn Bram over to Parisi." Sweet sounded more confident than he felt.

"I'm sorry, Sweet. That's not what I want but . . ."

"You have to check on me, right?"

Gypsy shrugged again. "It's what I do. We're checks and balances, me and you, right?"

"Always were," Sweet agreed. "God, he's fucked up, Gypsy."

Gypsy nodded. "Yep."

"Worse than Linc."

"Yep."

Sweet glanced at him. "No words of wisdom?"

"I seem to recall another guy who came here completely fucked up."

Sweet blinked at his friend—one of his best friends—and nodded. "Coming here saved you."

"You know it did. So what's the problem?" Gypsy asked. When Sweet didn't—couldn't—answer, Gypsy continued, "Because you're afraid you can't save him. And you want to, so badly, but you're willing to send him away rather than risk hurting him."

"Wow. Didn't realize you'd gone to shrink school."

"Don't ask shit you already know the answer to," was all Gypsy told him.

"Hey Bram? Bram."

Bram flailed and went to hit out, hard—when a strong hand grabbed his wrist. He opened his eyes and saw that his fist was inches away from Sweet's jaw. "Shit. Sorry."

"I came prepared."

He sat up as Sweet let go of his arm. "What time is it?" Because it still looked pitch-black out to him.

"Sun's almost up. Come on—get dressed. You need to check out something in the clubhouse."

Bram eyed him warily but Sweet just said, "It's okay."

"Is it about Linc?"

"We still don't know where he is. But we've cleared up some other stuff." Sweet paused. "I fucking hate how wary you are around me at times like this."

"Can you blame me?"

"No."

Bram nodded, went into the bathroom to piss, wash up, and brush his teeth. He dressed quickly, heart pounding, and followed Sweet the short distance from his cabin to the clubhouse.

Gypsy was there, and so were Tug and Ozzie and Boomer. They were sitting around the main table, waiting for him.

"Come sit," Sweet urged and Bram did so stiffly, wishing he had a knife . . . any kind of weapon.

As if reading his mind, Ozzie pulled a knife out of his pocket and slid it across the table to Bram. "That help?"

Bram wanted to laugh but he didn't. Instead, he took the knife and held it in his hand as Sweet started, "We think the best thing to do from here on out is to tell the Heathens that you're patching in here."

"I didn't— I don't think that's how it works," Bram said.

Sweet was honest with him. "Typically, it's not. But you're not a typical case. We're trying not to get into a war with the Heathens, and as long as you're here without being an MC member, the harder it gets to justify, even though they're not exactly our friends."

"I understand," Bram started, squeezing the handle of the folding hunting knife in his hand. "And that might work if Havoc takes me in as an abandoned Heathen probie. But once they find out I'm ATF, there's no deal."

"Good thing they'll never find out, then," Sweet told him.

Bram frowned. "How can you be sure?"

"Come with me," Sweet told him and brought him down into another section of the basement with more cells. Inside one of them was Parisi, bound and gagged, and Bram just stopped and stared . . . and then turned to look at Sweet to explain.

Which he did. "He admitted everything. He made a side deal with the Heathens. They have no idea either of you are ATF. And you were right—that account number? Ties Parisi to the Heathens."

"He confessed all that shit?" Bram asked.

"Got it on tape. Not sure we'll use it though," Sweet said meaningfully before letting Bram into the cell, advising, "Take your time with him, because once you're done? He's done."

Then he shut the door that led to the cells behind him.

For one brief, shining moment, Bram felt bad for Parisi . . . until he remembered how badly Parisi had set him up. "I want to hear what you told them," he said steadily, taking out Parisi's gag and giving him water to drink. "Start from the beginning and don't leave anything out."

"Of course. Bram, you have to understand—"

"I'll understand more when you start talking."

"Okay." Parisi took a breath and explained it all, how the Heathens presented a monetary opportunity Parisi couldn't pass up. That the money was free and clear. That it wouldn't have compromised the ATF mission.

That he deserved it after all those years with the ATF and zero glory. "Nothing, Bram. Nothing but 'Work harder.'"

"Yeah, nothing harder than sitting behind a desk listening to me getting beaten."

"It wasn't like that—"

"But it was. You sold me out so I wouldn't catch you."

Parisi sighed. "I got spooked. I admit it. But let me make it right."

"Tell me where Linc is."

"Linc? Your brother? I have no idea." Parisi looked genuinely confused.

Why wouldn't Parisi admit it? Use it as a bargaining chip if he knew? "I think the Heathens have him."

"They never said a word to me about that. They have no intel on you beyond thinking you're a probie who tried to bail. Your brother and sister aren't even in your classified file," Parisi reminded him.

"But you know about them."

Parisi sat back. "At this point, why wouldn't I share this with you? Let me talk to the Heathens though—if they do have him, I can—"

"No." Bram shook his head. He'd let it all sink in already and had no further use for listening. "Hey Sweet? I'm done here."

When Sweet came to the cell to let him out, Parisi begged, "Bram, you can't do this. It isn't you—this isn't who you are."

"Maybe I've turned into what you wanted me to be," was all Bram told him before brushing past Sweet and leaving Parisi . . . and probably the ATF behind for good. "Don't tell me anything more."

"Wasn't planning on it," Sweet assured him.

CHAPTER 24

HELL OR HIGH WATER

"**W**hat now, Sweet?" Bram asked as he watched the sun rise from Sweet's porch. He'd left the clubhouse before Sweet had, and now he didn't ask a damned question about Parisi or the asset.

Smart move. Smart man. "We've got a call to make. After we get some food."

An hour later, Bram was with Sweet in his office as he dialed the Heathen's clubhouse. The phone was on speaker and when Bones answered, Bram stiffened.

Sweet turned away and said, "Bones, it's Sweet. We need to talk."

When he heard the twangy drawl of, "Never thought we'd hear from you, Sweet. I'm guessing this is an apology for letting our probie hurt our MC the other night. If so, you should be down on your goddamned knees."

Bones had, very recently, gone from XO to the newly appointed president of the Heathens, a mean-as-all-fuck son of a bitch that Sweet had always wanted to kill with his bare hands for the sheer joy in watching himself do so.

Now, more than ever.

Sweet clamped down on his utter hatred and ground out, "Where is Linc?"

Bones gave a low, chilling laugh. "I didn't think he mattered much to you. Maybe to Geoff though . . ."

"Bones—"

"I'm still waiting on your apology. I'll get you on your knees sooner than later. Just like Geoff's little friend." Bones cut the connection, and Sweet pounded his hands on the desk at the black screen.

"Sweet, who the fuck is Geoff?" Bram was asking him, and Christ, he did not want to tell Bram any of this. Because he didn't want any of it to be true.

He pinched the bridge of his nose, squeezed it tight, and thought about dying. He could easily say to Bram, *He's no longer here and it's an old grudge—nothing to do with you*, and he wouldn't be (technically) lying.

But Bram wasn't the person Sweet was most worried about telling the truth to at the moment. "Geoff is Gypsy."

Bram frowned, and then, after a second, his eyes looked haunted. "It's . . . it's not me?" When Sweet shook his head, Bram whispered, "And Linc is his little friend . . . on his knees?"

Sweet didn't have to answer that. He put a hand on Bram's shoulder. "We'll get him back. He's alive, Bram."

"He's alive," Bram repeated, like he was trying to push away all the other horrible things he was picturing. After several seconds, he said, "This is going to kill Gypsy."

Sweet nodded. "I know." He put a hand on Bram's shoulder. "You have to know that Gypsy would never put Linc in the line of fire. Not with the Heathens. It's one thing to go after Linc for jumping bail, but he'd never . . ." Sweet felt his throat tightened. "It's such an old grudge—long forgotten. There've been other opportunities for them to . . ." He trailed off, because none of those opportunities had been as perfectly cutting as this one had proven to be.

But the upshot was, Linc was in trouble with the Heathens because of Havoc.

And Havoc could be in trouble with the Heathens because of Bram.

Fuck.

As if he knew exactly what Sweet was thinking—no doubt because he was thinking the same thing—Bram reached out and grabbed his biceps. "What the fuck are we going to do?"

"We're getting Linc back."

"I don't think we should tell Gypsy that Linc might be in there because of him," Bram said. "I'll shoulder the blame. After what Havoc's done for me, this should even us out."

Because Bram didn't want to owe Havoc—or anyone—anything. It angered Sweet and made him sad but at a level he understood. "That's not going to work, Bram. We both know that. Gypsy deserves to know the truth. He'll find out either way."

"So Gypsy was once a Heathen?"

Sweet stared at him. "Gypsy and Bones? They're brothers."

"Brothers or brothers?" Bram asked.

"At one time, both. Gypsy grew up in the Heathens."

Bram said quietly, looking stunned, "How's he been safe until now?"

"Havoc," Sweet said simply.

"So Heathens won't touch him because of that."

"Heathens are many things, but stupid when it comes to Havoc's ways? They don't fuck with that."

"Until now," Bram said quietly.

Sweet nodded. "Fuckers found a loophole."

"Why did Gypsy come here?"

"He didn't. At the time, he wanted no part of us at all. Some days, I believe he still doesn't." Sweet looked at him hard. "He reminds me a lot of you."

CHAPTER 25

IF YOU WANT BLOOD YOU GOT IT

Ten minutes after Sweet had talked to Bones, Gypsy walked into Sweet's office, a wary look in his eyes. "Ozzie said you needed me."

"Yeah." Sweet's drawl was low and raw and made Gypsy stiffen. Bram wondered if he knew instinctively what Sweet was about to tell him, or had he suspected this all along on some level?

Bram fought jumping to conclusions as Gypsy asked, "It's about Linc, isn't it?"

"Heathens have him," Sweet said without fanfare. "Bones hasn't admitted it, but he used your name. I wanted you to listen in when we called back."

"Skype him," Gypsy instructed, his voice hollow. "If he has Linc, he'll want to show him off."

"Gypsy—"

Gypsy cut Sweet off. "We both know what he'll want for a trade. But I want to hear him say it. I want proof of life."

Bram had watched the interaction silently until now. "You're going to trade me."

Sweet shook his head and Gypsy said, "He needs to stay out of this," acting like Bram wasn't in the room.

"You're kidding, right?" Bram said.

"Bram, they don't know you and Linc are brothers," Sweet reasoned.

"They also know that you have me here. They know you have Monk, their ex-probie. That's a trade they'll want. Trust me," Bram assured them.

"I can't let you do that, Bram," Gypsy said, finally addressing him.

"You're not letting me do anything. He's my brother."

"And this is my fault."

"We're on the same team here," Sweet reminded them. "Gypsy, at the least, let's let Bram bluff them."

Gypsy growled a little, but relented with a quick nod.

"Good. Both of you stay out of sight for now." Sweet motioned for them to move to the side of the computer, where he and Gypsy could see the screen but Bones wouldn't see them . . . and he rang Bones.

After several rings, Bones appeared on the screen, like he'd been waiting for this. Anticipating. "Figured you'd call back. I think I've got something of yours."

Bram's belly twisted with rage as he saw Linc. His mouth and nose were covered with a cloth but it was definitely Linc. Out of the corner of his eye, Bram saw Gypsy beginning to lunge toward the screen as if he could break through and save Linc from being waterboarded, and he grabbed Gypsy's arm hard, stopping him.

The man pouring water over Linc's face through the cloth stopped momentarily, pulled the cloth completely away so they could watch Linc's face contort in pain as he coughed, a hollow sound that rattled through their silent room.

"What do you want, Bones?" Sweet asked calmly.

"Tell Geoff to come home," Bones said crisply.

"It's been a long time—Heathens is no longer his home," Sweet reminded him.

"You never get over losing family," Bones said, and Bram, who watched the Skype session from the side, surrendered. For Gypsy, Linc, and Sweet.

For himself. "Take me instead."

Bones narrowed his eyes and then nodded. Bram had changed his voice to mimic Monk's heavy drawl but . . . "You look different, Monk."

"It's still me," Bram told him.

"We'll never stop coming for you," Bones assured him. "But for now, Geoff's who I want."

He motioned for the man to start waterboarding Linc again, and Bram watched helplessly as Linc struggled under the constant, steady flow of water. "I'll be there in a couple of hours if you stop that shit now."

"Why should I?" Bones asked.

"I have secrets I assume you don't want shared," Bram said, thinking about the overseas account—his only leverage. "I have accounting information. You kill me, it dies with me. You kill him . . ."

Bones stared at him with violence in his eyes, then nodded. He turned and told the man, "Stop," and they all watched Linc cough. Vomit. And then glare at the Heathens like he would kill them at the very first opportunity.

He'd turned into something dark during his kidnapping—he no doubt had to, in order to save himself.

Dammit.

"After your stunt the other night, we've escalated the process," Bones said. "We'd planned to keep Linc here longer, mainly because he really seems to be enjoying our hospitality."

"Fucker. Fuck you," Bram spat at the computer.

"Good to see you've recovered," Bones jeered. "I don't know why you're helping Havoc now, except to get back at us. But I'm a reasonable man, so I'm up for a trade."

"I'll be there," Bram growled.

"There'll be consequences," Bones warned him. "For the other night. For leaving us. And now, for threatening us. But I don't think Sweet would argue that a club needs consequences to keep its members in line. There are rules, and Sweet was always big on rules."

Sweet remained silent, but Bram noted the muscles in his jaw working overtime.

"Be here by four o'clock or the torture resumes," Bones told them. "And Geoff? Brother, you'll never be safe."

"He's scum," Bram said when Sweet cut the connection. "I'm taking him out."

"What happened to vengeance changing a man?" Sweet asked, without a trace of judgment.

"Like a wise man once told me, maybe I need changing," Bram said fiercely. "And Linc's okay. Pissed, but okay."

"Pissed is good. Means he'll fight," Sweet agreed.

But Gypsy . . . he stood there brokenly. "I don't like this choice."

"Me neither. But it has to be done. Please—just take care of Linc, no matter what he's like after all this. Fucking promise me," Bram demanded of both men.

Gypsy stared at him and nodded, and then he walked out. Bram went after him and Sweet didn't stop him.

"Gypsy . . ."

Gypsy stopped, squared his shoulders, and turned. "Must've been hell in there for you."

"Wasn't pretty. But it was a job, not my life," Bram said quietly. "It must've been true hell for you."

He wasn't sure what Gypsy would do with that but he finally nodded. "Yes"

"I'm sorry."

Gypsy held a hand up. "I think we both are." He paused. "Not many around here know about me."

"I'm damned good at secrets."

"Yeah. Guess you are." Gypsy nodded. "You can get out of there, Bram. I have faith in you. Don't you dare give up when you get in."

"I wasn't planning on it," Bram told him. But he'd also come to peace with the fact that he might not make it out of there alive.

CHAPTER 26

BAPTISM BY FIRE

"**Y**ou can't go alone—"

Bram held up his hand, resigned to the fact that he knew—that they both knew—that this conversation was both necessary and inevitable. "You can't go. You can't risk sending in Havoc or you'll escalate an all-out war. I'm not worth that."

"Bullshit," Sweet growled.

"You can't mean that," Bram told him. "This place is your whole life. You just met me—"

"And you've given a lot for this club."

"And brought a lot down on you too. You owe Linc, yeah, but I'm going in for him. Because Gypsy can't." Bram paused. "I think Gypsy loves him, if Gypsy's capable of loving anyone. He's more like me than I realized—he's right about that. But I have to do this alone."

Sweet turned away and stared out at the view from his porch. The lush green land seemed to vibrate with a truth even Bram could feel, and he was starting to understand why the men believed that Havoc land was as much a member of Havoc as they were.

"I can do this, Sweet. I do it for a living."

"This time, it's personal. I know from experience that personal can fuck up any mission."

Bram couldn't argue. "I'm going in. From there . . ."

"We'll be waiting close by."

"No backup comes inside," Bram said firmly. Sweet didn't say a word, and Bram figured that was the best he'd get.

After watching Bram take off in his truck, Sweet stared out at his land again and begged a silent plea, a prayer, to anyone or anything that was listening.

"I'd go in with him," Tug offered.

Sweet wasn't sure when he'd showed, but he was grateful for the sentiment. "I know."

"We all would, Sweet. Say the word," Tug continued. "I know Bram's got a death wish, but we could end this."

"And end up dead or in jail," Sweet reminded him. "It would be an all-out war—"

"Not if there aren't any Heathens left to tell the tale," Tug said, just as Ozzie's bike stormed up the hill. "Something's up."

Sweet agreed silently, and he and Tug strode out to meet Ozzie, who didn't turn his bike off before shouting, "Gypsy's gone."

"For how long?" Sweet demanded.

"No idea. He's not a prisoner. No one realized we had to keep him here," Ozzie said, but that wasn't exactly true. Even if most of Havoc didn't realize Gypsy's lineage, they knew Gypsy's relationship with Linc. All it would take was one word from Gypsy and they'd let him go get his revenge on Heathens.

"Who went with him?" Sweet asked.

"No one," Ozzie confirmed.

"Shit." Sweet fisted his hands and fought the urge to throw Ozzie off the bike and head into Heathens himself. In his younger days, he would've.

When you weren't president of Havoc. Now, he had a responsibility to the club to do things like not die.

"We'll go after him," Ozzie said. "Send me and Tug and Boomer. We'll stay quiet. Won't start anything. Just backup."

Sweet didn't hesitate to nod. "Put men at the gates. All of them. We have to keep Havoc safe." Then he paused for a long moment. "You don't know what you're walking into."

All three of the men going in had been in the military—two Marines and one Air Force. They'd been in life-or-death situations, and the two who stood before him were calm in their choice.

"We're good, Sweet," Tug assured him. "We'll get Gypsy. And if we can help Bram out—"

"Just go," Sweet told them. "And stay on the protected channel—I want constant contact."

The ride into Heathens was a long dirt road, a trip Bram dreaded every day he worked this job. Today, he sped up, dust kicking up behind him, and he cleared his mind of everything but getting Linc out. He had weapons. Flash bangs. Knives. If he was going down, it was only after Linc was safely out and he was taking as many Heathens with him as he could.

He expected to see Heathens out on the road waiting for him, but it was oddly deserted. As he got closer, he heard shouts. Saw flames. Wondered if they planned on burning him on the stake but quickly realized that the club members were too busy to even notice him.

That's when he saw Linc emerge from the bushes along the side of the road, limping toward his truck. He shoved the brakes on and went to get out to help Linc, who yelled, "Stay inside—I've got it."

Bram was halfway out when Linc managed to run toward the truck and get himself into the back seat. Bram looked to where Linc had come from and saw that the Heathens were starting to notice him, even as the flames from their compound shot higher into the air.

It wasn't the time for more revenge—someone had already taken that job on themselves.

"Please, Bram—get the hell out of here," Linc whispered.

Bram shut Linc's door and then got in and backed down the drive doing ninety. "Linc, talk to me."

"Tired, Bram. But I'm all right." A lie, but Linc was here. Safe. "Bones is dead."

"How?"

"I don't know. They think I did it. Fuck, I wish. But when the fire started, I was able to grab Bruno's keys." A long pause. "He's dead too."

"Good for you, Linc."

Linc's laugh was small and sarcastic. "Good for me. Yeah."

"Just hang on—I'll get you to the hospital. And I'm not leaving your side."

"Sweet, there's a shit-show going on out here." Ozzie's voice crackled across the secure line. "Heathens' compound is on fire."

"Any sign of Linc or Bram?" Sweet asked.

"Tug called Bram and it went to voice mail. There's no sign of Bram's truck or of Linc. All we know for sure is that Bones and Bruno are dead. Heathens are too busy putting out the fires to deal with much else."

Just then, a text from Misha came through.

Bram just brought Linc in. He's going to be okay.

"Bram's good—he got Linc to Misha," Sweet told them. "What about Gypsy?"

"No sign of him," Ozzie confirmed. "Want us to stick around watching or go in and add to the damage?"

Sweet was about to tell him to go in when he caught sight of a figure coming out of the woods, walking casually.

Gypsy.

Dammit. "Gypsy's back here. You all should get here too. This is just the beginning."

CHAPTER 27

IN THROUGH THE OUT DOOR

Misha met Bram and Linc at the ER, and Misha rushed Linc back into a curtained area, only allowing Bram to come back with them because Linc wouldn't let go of his hand.

"Linc, it's okay. She's good people," Bram told him. Linc nodded— he was zoned out on something, maybe overdosed, but he'd fought. There were wounds on his hands, and not only defensive ones. "You're safe."

"I know," Linc mouthed. "Are you?"

"Yes," Bram said with a confidence he didn't feel. It was enough to satisfy Linc, who surrendered his hand as long as Bram stayed close.

"I texted Sweet to let him know you're here," Misha said.

"Thanks. He needs to know," Bram said tiredly. He'd wanted to call Sweet but he'd also wanted to keep him at Havoc. Safe. "He's okay?"

"He's fine," Misha assured him as she grabbed the blunted scissors. She glanced up at him before she cut off Linc's clothes and Bram nodded, knowing what he'd see but refusing to look away. Linc was still awake—they wouldn't give him anything until his tox screen came back.

The cuts and bruises were consistent with beatings.

"He's got broken ribs and pneumonia," Misha confirmed, and Bram had feared the latter when he'd heard the rattle in Linc's chest.

"They waterboarded him," Bram murmured, and Misha raised her brows and then her expression tightened.

"Bastards." She ran her hand over Linc's forehead. "I'm going to put an IV in, okay? Just for an antibiotic and fluids. You've got enough drugs on board to keep you pain-free for a while. When they wear off, I'll give you something much different. Is that okay?"

Linc looked between her and Bram and nodded.

"Why don't you try to sleep? This is just oxygen." She showed him the nasal cannula and Linc nodded again, let her put the prongs into his nose. "I'm going to give you a treatment for your chest."

Linc had started to shiver. She asked the nurse for a warm blanket and got one. "Nothing on him now we can't take care of later. He doesn't need stitches. He needs rest."

Rest and relaxation. This time, he was the one who grabbed Linc's hand and wouldn't let go.

There would be blowback—Sweet anticipated it, prepared for it, and wasn't disappointed when the Heathens drove over the Shades Run border.

His men met them there, Sweet leading the pack. He'd forced Gypsy to remain inside and Gypsy hadn't given him any issues. Gypsy also wouldn't give him any goddamned answers about what happened over at Heathens, which really gave Sweet all the answers he needed.

He'd had to leave Bram and Linc at the hospital with Misha and a couple of Havoc men guarding. Ozzie, Tug, and Boomer were at his side. Heathens were going to get what was coming to them.

Parisi and his asset? They already had.

CHAPTER 28

AND THAT'S HOW IT IS
FOR A SOLDIER

The biker who edged into Linc's hospital room made Bram jump to attention. Even working on zero sleep, he had the guy pinned to the wall in seconds demanding, "Who the fuck are you?"

From behind him, he heard Linc whisper, "Jethro. Hey."

Jethro. Right. Bram had never met him in person, and for good reason. Undercover agents kept the lowest possible profiles in order to avoid accidental detection.

Still, Bram continued to stared at him until Jethro said, "Linc, can you call your bodyguard off?"

"He's cool, Bram," Linc said.

"Real fucking cool," Bram growled.

Jethro stared at him. "Havoc's fighting to keep Heathens out of Shades as we speak. I'm here for backup. It should be over soon."

Bram nodded and let him go, watched the big man with the dark-blue bandana wrapped around his head and a Hangmen MC vest go right up to the bed and take Linc's hand in his. "Hey kid. You hanging in there?"

"Much as I can." Linc glanced over at Bram. "That's my brother, Bram."

Jethro nodded at Linc and then slowly turned to Bram. "Heard a lot about you."

"I'll just bet," Bram muttered.

"You guys have something in common," Linc managed.

Bram narrowed his eyes. "Linc, did you call him here on purpose?" he demanded, but Linc's eyes closed, as they'd been doing, as per the strong painkillers being pumped into his system.

And even after all Linc had been through, he was still worried about Bram.

"Let's talk," Jethro suggested. He went to the door, looked out, then closed it and motioned for Bram to join him by the window. But not before he swept the room for bugs.

"I already did that."

"Bet you did." Jethro stuck his hand out. "Fellow Army."

"Good for you."

"You went into the ATF about three years after me," Jethro continued and Bram stared at him. "I've been undercover with the Hangmen for years now. I was under and alone for three years before they discovered who I was."

"And you lived to tell the tale?"

"Better than that. They left me alone. I was in to hang the Pagans, not the Hangmen, and that benefitted the Hangmen more than anything."

"How the fuck?" Bram sputtered.

"It's not easy," Jethro admitted to him. "I'm active—you're not. I'm alive by the grace of God and the Hangmen. I thought I was looking at a bullet in the head. But this lifestyle? It suits me. I can do my job and ride bikes. And I've done a damned lot of good for this town."

He had—Bram knew there was an agent on the inside helping to take down the Pagans, but he'd never imagined how deep undercover the guy would have to be. Thing was, he was looking at the real guy—what Jethro was doing wasn't an act.

"My dad rode for the Watchers," Jethro said, referencing a now-defunct club that had been folded into the Hangmen. "I had some damned fine memories. It was also my way into the Hangmen."

"You're close with them."

"Yep."

"And suppose they're committing crimes?"

Jethro shrugged. "They're not running drugs, guns, or women. They're not my job to police. I'm not doing anything illegal. That's the only way I can look at things."

It was using blinders to a large extent, but Bram could understand the justification. It wasn't like the ATF didn't go above the law in order to accomplish what they needed to. "So why are you telling me this?"

Jethro glanced at Linc. "Your brother? Always thinking about everyone else's happiness."

"He wants me to stay with Sweet. At Havoc."

"You planning on going back to the ATF?" Jethro asked.

"I'm cleared."

"Not what I asked," Jethro countered.

"Not sure it matters."

Jethro accepted that with a small nod and Bram wondered how much the biker had to do with clearing him. Whether he and Sweet had worked together to do the things Sweet had told him not to ask about. Right now, Bram had deniability.

He also had zero guilt about any of it.

Linc was refusing to see anyone but Bram—and Misha—and he'd accepted Jethro as well, but beyond that, he hadn't mentioned Gypsy. Sweet checked in, finally taking to texting because Bram wouldn't take his calls.

He told himself it was because he didn't want to bother Linc while he was resting, but in reality, Bram had no idea what to say to him.

But after a week, as Linc's physical heath improved, Sweet showed at the hospital. Bram had been bracing himself for it, but seeing Sweet's strong, handsome face made something dark and hot inside of him just need.

He didn't want to need. Not like that. "Let's walk," he said and Sweet nodded, followed him down the hall and the stairs until they hit a door that led to fresh air and privacy.

Bram breathed in, blinked up at the sun.

"I know Linc's improving," Sweet said. "Misha keeps me up."

"I know. I told her it was okay."

"What about you?" Sweet asked.

Bram laughed. "Me? Fuck. I don't even know. I mean, I didn't have time to process what I'd been through until now. But the shit I saw . . . fuck, I had to eat a lot of shit in my life, you know? You'd think I'd be used to it. But the Heathens? That was a whole new level. I thought I'd never climb out. Some days, I'm not sure I did."

"You did. You're out."

"Ah, Sweet, I'm just . . . done."

"What does that mean?"

Bram stared at the sky, then back at Sweet. "It means that I don't know who I really am anymore. I don't know if I ever knew—not truly. Maybe that's the problem. Maybe that's why undercover work was so appealing to me. Because I thought I'd find myself. Instead, I got pushed farther away."

"So what—you gonna go on a walkabout and find yourself?" It wasn't said with any kind of sarcasm.

"Maybe."

"Did you ever stop to think that the reason you're so good at undercover work is because you do know who you are? I think it takes a strong, sure personality as a base in order to pull off what you have."

Sweet really believed that of him. "That's . . . thanks for saying that."

"You know by now I don't say shit I don't mean."

Bram studied him. "You can't tell me it's been a cakewalk, being gay and out and in charge."

Sweet snorted. "Being in charge—gay or straight—getting to this point? The hardest challenge I faced. But Finn always told me it was my calling. He helped me come to terms with my sexuality. He was comfortable as fuck, so for me, it wasn't a big deal. Surprised the hell out of me when people gave a shit and acted like assholes. But I can fight."

Bram nodded. "So can I. But there are times . . . I want to stop."

"That first night—do you know why I brought the bartender along?" Sweet asked, and Bram shook his head. "Because I knew I'd get too goddamned attached to you if I didn't put something— someone else—between us. Could tell by what happened in the alley."

"Did it work?"

"Made it motherfucking worse," Sweet confessed.

At Sweet's words, Bram's eyes clouded. Shuttered.

Shit.

Sweet braced himself for the complete shutdown. But slowly, Bram looked at him and said, "I figured I was going to die that night. And I didn't give a shit. I'm not saying I wouldn't have fought but . . ."

"You had a death wish," Sweet finished, realizing for the first time how Bram had let himself be with a member of an MC when he was hiding from other bikers—and had almost been killed by them.

Bram had made the first move. Had he wanted Sweet to kill him in that alley? Or had he merely expected it?

"Babe." He took Bram's chin in his palm. "I guess there was a lot about that first night neither of us knew."

"But now we do."

"But now we do." Sweet realized he could break this man with one wrong move, and he was far too aware of it now to ever let it happen again.

And you're going to fuck it up. Again.

No. With Jimmy-Boy, it was Sweet being selfish, but this time, it was about saving Bram from his demons and letting Bram save himself. "Go with Linc. Take care of him." When what he'd really meant was, *Let him take care of you.*

What he really wanted to say was, *Stay with me.*

But the damage was done. Needed to be.

"You want me to go," Bram said, like he was repeating it so Sweet could confirm.

"We can't . . . you said yourself it won't work."

"And you said it could. That it was me holding it back."

Sweet couldn't answer that, just told him, "This doesn't mean Havoc's abandoning you. We can patch Linc in. You too. Or—"

"Or we run," Bram finished.

"Even if you leave . . . you can still be protected by Havoc. You can still be Havoc."

"Now who's using a shield?" Bram shook his head hard. "We'll take our chances without you."

"Bram—"

"You made your point earlier."

"I won't let you risk your life."

"Guess what? That's not something you're in charge of anymore. You've got nothing to hang over my head. My secrets almost got you killed, and yours and Gypsy's? They almost killed Linc. So this makes us even."

"Bram . . ."

Bram turned stone-faced. "You want me gone because you can't deal with it? You think I ever let myself believe you could?"

He didn't give Sweet time to answer that . . . and Sweet wouldn't have. For Bram's own good.

Bram finally barked, "Go, Sweet. I'll leave your family alone if you get the fuck out of here and leave mine alone."

Sweet stared into Bram's eyes one last, quick time. And then he did what Bram told him to.

CHAPTER 29

ALL SCREWED UP

Gypsy wasn't seeing anyone. Holed up on the north side of the compound, he stayed inside. Food was dropped to him on his front porch. His garbage was put out. Otherwise, no one talked to him. Tug took over the bonds shop.

Sweet had no other choice but to run the club like a machine, even though his brain was on autopilot. Rush and Ryker came back, and Rush went to stay with Linc and Bram for a while, with Havoc's blessing.

"I know where they are," Ryker offered Sweet.

"Good," Sweet said hollowly. "I'm worried about Gypsy."

"Me too. But I'm equally worried about you."

"Don't. It's for the best."

Ryker crossed his arms and stared his president down. "Why's that? Because you decided it? Because you forced him out for his own good?"

"Yes, dammit. Yes to all of that," Sweet told him fiercely. "This life . . . I won't be the one who breaks him."

"You wouldn't."

"I did. For a moment, I did. You didn't see him, Ryker. You didn't see him."

"At one point, Rush was him. So I've seen it, Sweet."

"Just because it worked for you doesn't mean it'll work for me." Sweet shook his head. "Just . . . be there for Bram and Linc until they decide what to do. That's all I need."

Ryker wisely said nothing more. For the first time, Sweet wished someone would buck harder against him.

Linc insisted Bram rent them a house on the lake. Because that was the thing about memories. While Bram's were of a terrified nature when it came to anything water related, Linc's were more centered on the adventure of almost drowning, of his big brother saving him.

So of course, Bram caved. Rented the house about an hour from Shades, but keeping that town squarely in between them and the Heathens. Linc also needed to stay close to the hospital for regular checkups, and he'd grown too fond of Misha for him to give her up.

Rush visited, bringing Ryker with him, and Bram had stayed away, not wanting to see anything Havoc related.

When he returned, their Harleys were gone and he found Linc down by the lake, staring at the water, just like he used to when they were kids.

They were both men now, both knew how to swim . . . and they were still both fucking drowning.

"Good visit?" he asked, sitting down next to his brother and letting his feet dangle into the water.

"Yeah." There were circles under his eyes. "Rush is happy. Deserves to be."

"So do you."

Linc snorted. "Thanks, Dr. Bram. Right back at you." Then he shrugged. "Rush said Gypsy won't talk to anyone. He doesn't work. He's just holed up in his place at Havoc."

"Yeah, that's what Sweet told me too."

"I called him, you know." Linc glanced up at Bram. "Gypsy, not Sweet. I left him a message. And I waited by the phone like a lovesick girl waiting for him to call me back. Hell, I figured banning him from the hospital would make him want to come see me even more but . . ."

But. "Do you remember anything about your rescue?"

Linc shook his head. "It's a blur. Still. Misha said it will probably come back to me."

"She told me that too." Bram knew that Gypsy had been there. He wasn't supposed to tell Linc any of it though, because Misha said that was like planting memories. Still, if it gave Linc comfort to know that Gypsy had been an integral part of his rescue . . .

Dammit.

"It's okay I guess," Linc continued. "Gypsy and I . . . well, how far could it have gone, you know? If it had legs, he'd be here."

"He's got guilt, Linc. Even though it's not his fault."

"Technically it is." Linc stared, a haunted look Bram had never wanted to see in his eyes, and again, the anger rose inside of Bram. "I heard them say that they promised Gypsy that they'd take his happiness away. I guess Gypsy didn't consider me like that. I was only sleeping with him for a few weeks. It wasn't like we were serious . . ."

"You're right. He should've warned you somehow," Bram told him. "But you made him happy. Trust me."

"Such a fucking crime to be happy," Linc muttered. "I can't believe Bones is Gypsy's brother."

Bram nodded. "I thought it was my fault, you know. The whole time . . ."

"I'm sorry."

"No apologies. From now on, contact. Constant."

Linc rolled his eyes and sighed. "Great." But there was a smile too. "So what now? Tied at the hip and where do we go?"

Bram was aware that Linc watched him wrestle with the question. Finally, Bram offered, "We could run."

"Yeah, we could," Linc said, tiredness sounding like it threatened to envelop him, the way it had whenever he thought about anything Havoc—and Gypsy—related. A stress reaction for sure. "But the running part . . ."

"You know where we're safest. It's not about Havoc's compound. It's about becoming members." Bram's voice sounded as hollow as the look in his brother's eyes.

"Right. Full-time protection," Linc said tiredly.

Gypsy had to suspect what the Heathens had done to him. Bram learned it from the docs who took care of Linc in the hospital and Linc? Well, he'd lived it, and although he refused to talk about it, Bram knew he'd have to, sooner or later, or it would take him down. "Gypsy didn't know, Linc."

"He didn't make a move to find me, though. He was looking for his money." Linc spoke as if stating a fact—there was no anger behind it. That was the problem though—there was no feeling at all. "I'm always going to remind him of his past now, and I'm guessing it's not a past he wanted anyone to know about. So I can't go to Havoc and stay there, Bram. I can't, but you can," Linc told him finally.

"Let them put you under protection."

"No."

"Then let me," Bram said fiercely.

"Let you what?"

"If I patch in, you're family. Protected. They won't touch you."

Linc gave a short, humorless laugh. "Ah, Bram, they won't touch me anyway," he said, the honesty a brutal blow he'd already dealt to himself from day one. "They already got their satisfaction—they ruined him and they ruined me. The damage? It's me, and it's done and it's permanent."

Even though Linc kept his voice as emotionless and as matter-of-fact as he could, Bram still knew the depths of his pain. Knew, moved in, and closed him arms around him, unsurprised when Linc began to sob for the first time since escaping his ordeal.

Bram just held on, and he wasn't sure how long it took for Linc to let it all out. But when he finally had—for the moment, at least—Linc pulled away, wiped his eyes, and looked at Bram.

Bram spoke first. "I know you believe everything you said. But I'm going to do everything I can to help you, to not make it true."

Linc nodded. "I still think— Havoc—"

"Linc, if I'm in . . . I'm always a reminder."

"Bram, do you think that if you're not a Havoc member, I'll magically forget?"

Bram shook his head helplessly.

"Go to him. Go to Sweet."

"He told me to stay away, Linc. Said it's not going to work. I know I remind him too much of his ex, who died in combat. He wants to keep me out of danger. Or something. I tried to push back but it just made things worse."

"And you think he meant it?" Linc asked.

"Sweet usually says what he means."

"*Riiight.*" Linc stretched out the word and rolled his eyes. "Like he's not trying to make sure you're safe. He knew you'd be torn between staying with me and staying with him."

"How'd you get so damned smart?"

"I listened to my older brother, even when he thought I wasn't." Linc patted him on the shoulder. "Go to him. I'll be here. I'm staying here for a bit. Rush said he'll come stay with me until it's time for me to go, okay? He and Ryker just went to go get something to eat until I talked to you about it."

Bram stared at his brother. "Trying to get rid of me so soon?"

"No way. I just need to figure some things out, okay? I'm fine— I'll be in touch. I just . . . I don't know, Bram. I don't know anything anymore."

"Don't run."

"I won't be running this time. I'll be trying to piece myself back together. I need to. You know that."

"Yeah, I do."

"I'll be all right. You'll be too. Because you're a good man, Bram. All those times you've been going undercover? Hate to break it to you, but you're still you. You're not trying to escape yourself as much as you're trying to self-protect."

Bram wanted to push Linc into the lake but, just like the asshole somehow knew, he rolled over and let himself half fall, half dive into the placid water. Because, if nothing else, Linc was too stubborn and zen to have a fear of water after his near-drowning. Instead, Bram watched as his brother's head emerged, as sleek as a seal disrupting the smooth surface and redirecting the ripples.

Because that? That was Linc.

"Hate it that you're right," Bram muttered, and as though Linc heard, he turned, smiled, and dove under again.

This time, Bram joined him.

CHAPTER 30

I CAN'T QUIT YOU BABY

Bram got into his truck and drove toward Havoc, passing Rush and Ryker in the lake house's driveway. That made him feel marginally better about leaving Linc behind, but his little brother didn't know that Bram would be a frequent visitor as long as Linc stayed there.

Or stayed anywhere. Bram would just keep racking up those miles.

As he made the two-hour drive, he got mad at himself, but even madder at Sweet.

"For my own good. Asshole fucker thinks he can trick me," he said out loud as the realization washed over him. "He'll have to try harder."

Sweet was sitting on his front porch when Tug's bike stopped in front of the house and Tug called, "Hey—your boy just drove his bike up the hill. Almost went through the night watchmen, but they jumped out of the way last minute." And sounded a little too smugly happy about it.

"Then what fucking good are they?" Sweet yelled.

"They saw who it was. Didn't really see the need to risk their lives to keep Bram away from you."

"Fuck that. I'll kill them myself. And for the record, Bram's not my . . ." He trailed off as they heard Bram's truck tearing up the roads, coming closer.

"Sweet? You were saying?" Tug prompted.

"Fuck off."

"Right. That's what I thought. Have fun," Tug offered as he prepared to roar off. "And this shit right here? This is why I'm single."

"You're single because no woman will put up with your ass for more than a night," Sweet yelled to him as he pulled away.

Then he waited, camped out, arms crossed. But Bram never came any closer . . . at least not to his house. No, he heard the fucker's truck zooming along the road behind his house and veering off toward the clubhouse instead.

Did the guys cover for him, leading Bram to the wrong place? And why did that make Sweet angry?

He paced the porch for a while, listening to the music blaring from the clubhouse, swore he wasn't going over there. But an hour later, Bram's truck was still there and no one had contacted him about trouble.

Would they have? Was Bram in trouble?

Fuck it. He walked over to the clubhouse and went inside. The party was in full swing, with MC members and their guests packing the bar and the pool room. And that's where Sweet found Bram, who was standing there talking to Ozzie, beer in hand. And laughing.

I'll give you something to laugh about . . .

He couldn't tear his eyes off Bram. He'd gained weight—good weight. His skin was tan, his eyes clear. They became laser-focused when he spotted Sweet but he didn't move, content to let Sweet come over to him.

Bastard. Who did this guy think he was? He marched toward Bram, finally getting close enough to say, "Who gave you an open invite here?"

Bram raised his brows and Ozzie said, "I did. So did Tug. Boomer. Oh, and—"

"Forget it. I don't need the list." He glared at Ozzie, who shrugged and excused himself. The music seemed to get louder and he moved in closer to Bram.

"Anything you'd like to say to me?" Sweet demanded.

"Actually yes." Bram took a long pull from his beer, then put the bottle down on the pool table, leaned into Sweet, and growled, "Don't you ever try to get rid of me for a bullshit, made-up reason again. Hear me?"

Sweet stared at him for a long moment before he found his voice. Finally, he blinked and told Bram, "Don't ever tell me what to do unless my cock's in you."

Bram smiled. The most beautiful, heart-melting smile Sweet had ever seen.

The *bastard*.

"Fuck that. You know I'll break that rule over and over. And you know you're counting on that," Bram told him. "Because you love me. Because I love you, Sweet."

Even as the pleasure of Bram's words washed over his goddamned cynical-as-shit heart, Sweet forced himself to glare at him. "Your ass is mine."

Bram smiled. "About fucking time you remembered that."

"Yeah, about fucking time," Sweet echoed, a gentle palm on Bram's cheek.

After Sweet touched his cheek, he yanked Bram in for a kiss. Bram was aware of cheering around them, but Sweet wasn't letting him up for air.

Bram wasn't complaining, not even when Sweet got him onto his back on the pool table in the middle of the room that was crowded with MC members, many of whom had already partied so hard they didn't know their own names. Most of them were in their own world of inebriation and the person they'd chosen to spend the night with. Bram noted several women being fucked on the bar—some of them were what Sweet referred to as *the mamas*, and a few men were fooling around with their old ladies unabashedly.

Sweet said that public sex was pretty common around here, but once a couple got serious, the majority of the sex happened away from the group.

So Bram was ready—and not ready—when Sweet bent him so his back was flat on the felt surface. His legs had nowhere to go but around Sweet's waist for quarter. Sweet hovered over him, leaning on his palms on either side of Bram's head as he kissed him while rocking against him, their jean-clad cocks rubbing against each other.

The friction was enough to drive Bram over the edge if he'd let it—and he knew Sweet liked that. But it was so motherfucking public. And even though this was Sweet's club, and the men were obviously fine with Sweet being gay, there was something to be said about being so open in such a fiercely, traditionally heterosexual environment.

He felt watched, which usually turned him on in the gay clubs. Here, he was on display, the prize of the president intent on showing Bram off to everyone.

Did he matter enough to stop at just kissing? Would Sweet strip him down here, like Bram was one of the mamas who didn't expect to be fucked in private?

While the thought excited him in the realm of fantasy, it would only continue to if it remained solidly in that realm and didn't become a reality.

But really, Bram wanted Sweet—wouldn't fight him, because he was beyond that, too far gone. He wanted Sweet with a fierceness that grew stronger by the day, and he forced the thought that he didn't mean much more to Sweet than a transient woman out of his head. It was the only way he could survive this moment, this night . . . this entire experience.

Because Sweet was reaching between Bram's legs, unzipping his jeans and easing them down Bram's hips. Bram kept his eyes closed, kept kissing Sweet, letting him lead, following his pace.

"Gonna let me in, babe?" Sweet asked against his ear as he fingered Bram, who'd never felt more exposed in his life. His body shuddered—anticipation and nerves bundled together, and his only answer was a moan, then a nod.

He didn't see Sweet's reaction, because he kept his eyes closed and his face buried in Sweet's neck, but Sweet's fingers were wet and slippery with lube, and they stroked his hole, eased him open carefully.

What the fuck did all of this look like? Bram could only imagine, and that made him blush and get harder all at once. And fuck, he'd long outgrown the shy, retiring act.

"I might want you to suck me off—will you do that right now?" Sweet's words washed over him. His skin tightened, heated, and again, he nodded with his eyes screwed tightly shut. "Yeah, you would. But maybe I'll just fuck you instead. Ready for me?"

When he nodded, Sweet ordered, "Say it. Tell me to fuck you. Tell me you want it."

Shit. He opened his mouth, not sure anything would come out, but Sweet's cock brushed his hole, then slid back and forth along his crack as Sweet stroked Bram's cock. "Christ—yes. Fuck me, Sweet—come on—right now. Don't tease."

Sweet chuckled, then slid inside of Bram without warning, without easing himself in. Bram stilled at the sudden fullness, then groaned, "Yeah, that's it," loud enough for him to hear himself over the music. "So good."

But still, he couldn't totally give himself over to the pure pleasure, kept his face hidden against Sweet's neck, like that could hide him completely.

And Sweet knew it, had obviously known it the entire time because he told Bram, "Babe, we're alone. It's all right. Been alone since before I took your jeans down."

Bram didn't believe him even as Sweet's words bored their way into his heart, past the barriers he'd built up over the years to prevent that very goddamned thing from happening. The music still pounded around them, although not as bone-crushingly loud as it had been. When Sweet moved his mouth down Bram's neck and sucked, Bram forced his eyes open and saw that the lights were dimmed and that they were indeed utterly alone in a room that had been full of partiers not ten minutes before.

"How?" he managed.

Sweet glanced up at him. "I have my ways. Pays to be in charge."

"I thought—"

"I know. And you would've done it anyway," Sweet told him. It wasn't an accusation, merely a calm statement of fact Bram agreed with wholeheartedly. He'd surrendered to Sweet's wants, his needs . . . he'd shown the other MC members that Sweet was not only in charge of the club, but in charge of his man. And in this culture, that was possibly the most important sign of an effective leader.

He'd trusted Sweet, and Sweet hadn't let him down.

And finally, Bram could say the same about himself. And as he accepted Sweet's thrusts, taking the hard strokes of cock against gland, he came as Sweet murmured, "Love you, Bram," over and over against Bram's cheek.

Explore more of the *Havoc Motorcycle Club* series at:
riptidepublishing.com/collections/series-havoc

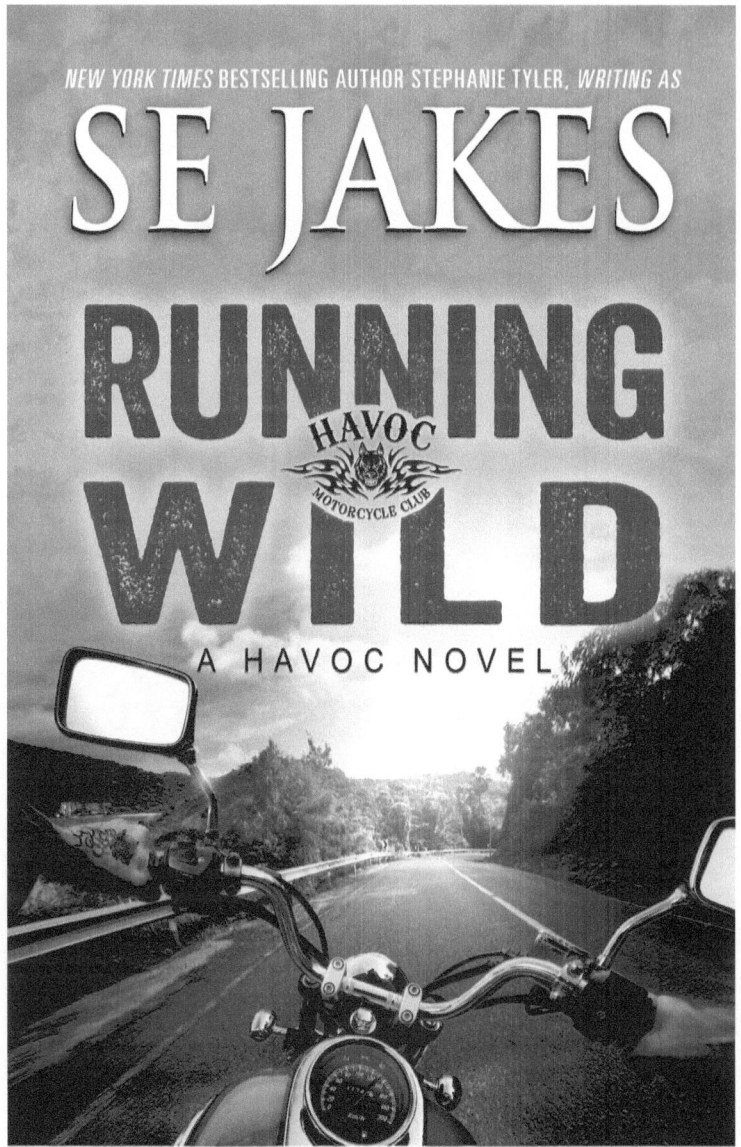

NEW YORK TIMES BESTSELLING AUTHOR STEPHANIE TYLER, *WRITING AS*

SE JAKES

RUNNING

HAVOC
MOTORCYCLE CLUB

WILD

A HAVOC NOVEL

Dear Reader,

Thank you for reading SE Jakes's *Running Blind*!

We know your time is precious and you have many, many entertainment options, so it means a lot that you've chosen to spend your time reading. We really hope you enjoyed it.

We'd be honored if you'd consider posting a review—good or bad—on sites like **Amazon, Barnes & Noble, Kobo, Goodreads, Twitter, Facebook, Tumblr,** and your blog or website. We'd also be honored if you told your friends and family about this book. Word of mouth is a book's lifeblood!

For more information on upcoming releases, author interviews, blog tours, contests, giveaways, and more, please sign up for our weekly, spam-free newsletter and visit us around the web:

> **Newsletter**: riptidepublishing.com/newsletter
> **Twitter**: twitter.com/RiptideBooks
> **Facebook**: facebook.com/RiptidePublishing
> **Goodreads**: tinyurl.com/RiptideOnGoodreads
> **Tumblr**: riptidepublishing.tumblr.com

Thank you so much for Reading the Rainbow!

RiptidePublishing.com

ACKNOWLEDGMENTS

As always, it takes a village, and mine includes Rachel Haimowitz, May Peterson, Alex Whitehall, L.C. Chase (another gorgeous cover!), and everyone else at Riptide who helps to ensure my releases go smoothly.

Also, to my readers who understood my (unplanned and unexpected) hiatus and hung in there, and to my family, who I couldn't do this without. More to come, and I hope you all enjoy Bram and Sweet as much as I did!

ALSO BY SE JAKES

Havoc Motorcycle Club
Running Wild
Running on Empty (Coming
soon)

Hell or High Water (EE, Ltd.)
Catch a Ghost
Long Time Gone
Daylight Again
Not Fade Away
If I Ever (Coming soon)

Men of Honor
Bound by Honor
Bound by Law
Ties That Bind
Bound by Danger
Bound for Keeps (EE, Ltd.)
Bound to Break

Phoenix, Inc.
No Boundaries

Standalone
Free Falling (EE, Ltd.)

Dirty Deeds (EE, Ltd.)
Dirty Deeds
Dirty Lies (Coming soon)
Dirty Love (Coming soon)

Inked
Hold The Line
Thirds

ABOUT THE AUTHOR

SE Jakes writes m/m romance. She believes in happy endings and fighting for what you want in both fiction and real life. She lives in New York with her family and most days, she can be found happily writing (in bed). No really . . .

SE Jakes is the pen name of New York Times best-selling author Stephanie Tyler (and half of Sydney Croft).

You can contact her the following ways:

Email: authorsejakes@gmail.com

Instagram: instagram.com/authorstephanietyler

Website: sejakes.com

Tumblr: sejakes.tumblr.com

Facebook: Facebook.com/SEJakes

Twitter: Twitter.com/authorsejakes

Goodreads Group: Ask SE Jakes

Truth be told, the best way to contact her is by email or in blog comments. She spends most of her time writing but she loves to hear from readers!

Enjoy more stories like
Running Blind
at RiptidePublishing.com!

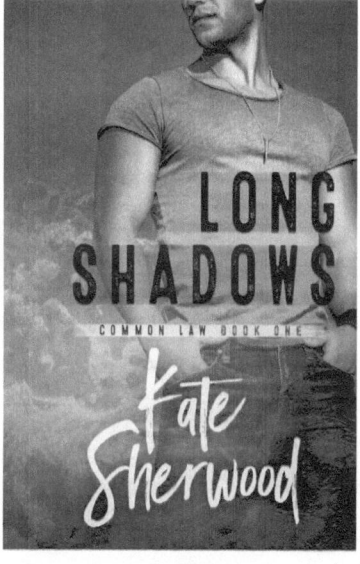

Kill Game

Long Shadows

The deck is not stacked in their favor with this game-playing killer.

Sometimes a bad decision is so much better than a good one.

ISBN: 978-1-62649-526-5

ISBN: 978-1-62649-620-0

www.ingramcontent.com/pod-product-compliance
Lightning Source LLC
Chambersburg PA
CBHW030113030726
47498CB00007B/2366